She stared at h
peration.

At last she said, 'I su
home with me.'

'You mean you have room in this apartment of
yours on the seafront at Cowes?'

He was mocking her now and she knew it. 'It's
a two-bedroomed apartment,' she said tightly,
pushing her plate away, her meal only half-eaten,
as she got to her feet.

'I didn't for one moment imagine it was anything
else,' he said solemnly. 'I somehow couldn't
believe, on such short acquaintance, you would
be inviting me to share your bed.'

Laura MacDonald lives in the Isle of Wight, and is married with a grown-up family. She has enjoyed writing fiction since she was a child, but for several years she worked for members of the medical profession, both in pharmacy and in general practice. Her daughter is a nurse and has helped with the research for Laura's medical stories.

FROM THIS
DAY FORWARD

BY
LAURA MACDONALD

MILLS & BOON®

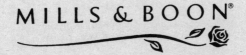

*First published in Great Britain 1998
Harlequin Mills & Boon Limited,
Eton House, 18-24 Paradise Road, Richmond, Surrey TW9 1SR*

© Laura MacDonald 1998

ISBN 0 263 80771 1

*Set in Times 10 on 12 pt. by
Rowland Phototypesetting Limited
Bury St Edmunds, Suffolk*

03-9804-46887-D

*Printed and bound in Great Britain
by Mackays of Chatham PLC, Chatham*

CHAPTER ONE

IF KATE CHAPMAN hadn't been late for afternoon surgery she might just have given a second glance to the rather scruffy stranger who sat in the corner of the crowded waiting room. As it was, she hardly noticed him, only pausing briefly at the reception desk on the way to her consulting room.

'I'm here, Claire,' she called to the younger of the two receptionists on duty. 'Give me a couple of minutes, then send the first one in.'

'Oh, yes, right, Dr Chapman,' said Claire. As Kate breezed away down the passage the girl leaned across the desk and breathlessly added, 'Oh, Doctor, there's someone to see you. . .'

'Not now, Claire,' called Kate over her shoulder. 'Later. . .'

Kate was the most junior of the partners at the Fleetwood Centre but she considered her room was one of the nicest, if not *the* nicest in the entire practice. Large and airy, it looked out across acres of woodland and meadows with glimpses of the sea in the distance through the trees.

Kate dumped her medical case on the floor and shrugged out of her navy blue jacket, hanging it on the hook behind the door. Glancing in the mirror above the washbasin in the corner of her room, she sighed as she caught sight of her wind-swept appearance, attempted briefly to tidy her dark hair, then sat down at her desk and pulled the pile of patient records towards her. She only had time to register that the records on top of the pile were those of Harry Turner when there came a tap at her door.

'Come in.' She looked up as the door opened and Harry Turner's daughter, Helen, came into the room.

'Helen,' said Kate, 'I thought it must be you and not Harry. Come in and take a seat.'

'Thanks, Kate.' Helen sat down. 'You're quite right, of course. I'm afraid the days are becoming few and far between now when Dad can get to the surgery.'

'So, how is he?' Kate was faintly alarmed by Helen's appearance. They'd been friends since their schooldays but rarely had she seen her looking so tired.

'There's no change, really. But, then, I'm not expecting any miracles. Alzheimer's takes its steady toll, I'm afraid.' Helen sighed. 'It's hard, standing by and watching someone deteriorate, but there it is. I guess I'm not the only one it's happened to, and I certainly won't be the last.'

'I'll always come and visit if you need me to,' said Kate.

'I know you will, and I'm grateful for that,' said Helen. 'But all I need at the moment is his repeat prescriptions, and to discuss his medication with you.'

'Right.' Kate turned to her computer and brought Harry Turner's medication chart to the screen. The next few minutes were spent adjusting doses and the strengths of his heart medication, antidepressants, muscle relaxants and laxatives.

When Kate had finished she pressed the print button, and while the prescriptions were being printed, she turned back to Helen. 'Don't forget,' she said, 'when the day comes that you really can't cope at home, you must say, and we'll talk about some alternative care.'

'I think I'm all right for the time being,' said Helen slowly. 'I really do dread the thought of him having to go into full-time care, but I know the time will come. The day unit is still coping with him at the moment but he is becoming increasingly erratic. Twice last week he wandered off and they had to call me from work. The second time he had somehow got all the way to Cowes. He was on the parade, watching the yachts—goodness knows how he got there.'

'He misses his sailing,' said Kate.

Helen nodded. 'On the other hand, I find he gets very agitated if there is a lot of noise or people around. For that reason I have decided not to let the stable flat this season. I don't think he could cope with children being around, which is such a shame when you consider how much he once loved family life. Even my sister's family were too much for him at Christmas. . .'

'So, are you saying your flat is empty?' asked Kate suddenly.

'At the moment,' Helen replied, 'but I've promised it to my cousin's daughter, Siobhan, just until she gets a place of her own. She's training for the paramedics at the moment.'

'Oh, I see.'

'Why did you ask?'

'Oh, nothing, really. It's just our new locum,' Kate replied. 'He's arriving in a few days and it's been left to me to find him somewhere to live. I must confess I haven't got round to doing anything about it yet. It won't be an easy task on the Isle of Wight, with the season coming along.'

'You can say that again,' Helen replied, adding thoughtfully, 'Who is he exactly—anyone we know?'

Kate shook her head. 'No. Someone by the name of Jonathan Hammond. Apparently, he owes Paul Wooldridge a favour and has agreed to do part of his sabbatical year for him.'

'So, what happened to your last locum—Simon Phillips, wasn't it?' asked Helen.

'He's gone back to Oxford to take up a new post,' Kate replied. 'He could only do three months for us. It's a shame, really, he was so nice. We'd all just got used to him and now we're back at square one.'

'Where does he come from, this Dr Hammond?' Helen tucked the prescriptions into her bag.

'I don't really know where his home is, but he's been working with the Voluntary Overseas Service in Africa. According to Paul, he's been on leave in this country after contracting some tropical virus. He's recovered, but they won't let him return immediately so he's agreed to fill in with some locum work until he goes back.'

'Well,' said Helen slowly, 'Siobhan won't be here for some time, probably not until May or early June. Tell you what, let me meet this guy when he arrives. We'll see what we can work out, even if it is only temporary.'

'Thanks, Helen, I really would appreciate it,' said Kate gratefully. 'And I can't imagine that having him around would pose too much of a problem for you.'

'Well, it certainly won't be the same as having a family with young children staying in the flat.' Helen stood up. 'I must get along. I'm on duty, really. I've just popped out in my break to get these.'

'So how is Accident and Emergency?' asked Kate with a smile as she pressed the buzzer for the next patient.

'The same as it always is.' Helen opened the door, paused and looked back. 'Busy and chaotic—but I love it.'

'Well, don't go overdoing it. . .' Kate trailed off as the intercom flashed and Claire's voice came through.

'Dr Chapman,' she said, 'Dr Hammond has arrived. He's in Reception.'

'Good heavens!' exclaimed Kate. 'We weren't expecting him until the end of the week. Thank you, Claire,' she added. 'I'll come through.' She pulled a face at Helen. 'Talk of the devil,' she said.

Getting to her feet, she joined Helen and as they stepped out into the corridor she said, 'At this rate, I doubt I'll ever get this surgery done. But at least this could be a chance for you to see your potential new lodger.'

'I'm afraid I really don't have the time to stay now,' said Helen swiftly. 'Tell you what, why don't you bring him over this evening? Then he can see the flat. Afraid he wouldn't be able to move in for a couple of days or so—we've got the painters in—but bring him over, anyway.'

'Thanks,' said Kate, 'I will, and I could see Harry at the same time.'

As they walked into Reception Kate immediately caught sight of the new locum. He was standing by the desk, joking with the receptionists. Dressed in an immaculate pin-striped navy suit with a crisp white shirt and patterned tie, his short dark hair was gelled to give it the fashionable 'wet look'. His smile, as Kate and Helen approached, was devastating—a flash of strong, white teeth in a tanned face.

He looks like a Jonathan, thought Kate, while Helen murmured behind her hand, 'Where do you find them? See you later.' With that she was gone, back to her duties at the Shalbrooke Hospital next door to the Fleetwood Centre, leaving Kate to greet her new colleague.

'Dr Hammond, I presume?' With a smile and an out-stretched hand, she stepped forward. Her hand was taken in a firm handshake and the smile grew wider, but at the same time there was a faintly bemused look in the blue eyes.

'I appreciate the welcome,' he said, 'but I fear there is some misunderstanding.'

'Really?' Kate frowned and glanced at the receptionists but for the moment both girls were engaged with taking phone calls. 'I don't understand,' she said. 'I was told Dr Hammond was here.'

'Sorry to disappoint you.'

'You aren't Dr Hammond?'

'I only wish I were.' The expression was rueful now but he still held her hand. Leaning forward slightly in a rather conspiratorial manner, he added, 'I'm from Harland Pharmaceuticals—Gregory Sumpter. If you could spare me a little time, Dr Chapman?'

Kate withdrew her hand smartly. 'I'm sorry, Mr Sumpter, it seems there's been some sort of mistake. Do you have an appointment?'

The man shook his head and with his hand on his heart said, 'Regretfully, no, but—'

'We only see medical reps by appointment,' said Kate crisply. 'If you'd like to have a word with Claire or Jackie, I'm sure they'll make arrangements for you to be seen after morning surgery tomorrow.'

With a quick, puzzled glance around the waiting room at the remaining patients, none of whom remotely resembled Kate's expectation of a locum GP, she leaned over the desk again and as Claire came off the phone she said, 'I understood Dr Hammond was here, Claire.'

'Oh, yes, he is,' Claire replied. 'He's over there...'
She nodded across the room.

Kate swung round and stared in the direction that Claire
was indicating. All she could see was a figure that was
sitting, or rather lounging, on a chair beneath the window.
Long legs which ended with huge black boots and were
encased in faded blue jeans were thrust out in front of
him and crossed at the ankles. His arms were folded, his
chin was on his chest and a dark green waxed hat with a
wide brim was pulled so far forward it almost covered
his face.

'Doctor,' called Claire, giving Kate no time for speculation, 'Dr Hammond.'

The figure stirred, pushed back the hat, opened one eye
and peered across the room at Kate and Claire.

'Dr Hammond, this is Dr Chapman,' said Claire breathlessly.

The man stood up, stretched, pushed the hat to the back
of his head, revealing shaggy, fair hair bleached by the
sun, and then, with no sense of urgency, ambled forward.

'Hi, Kate,' he said. 'Jon Hammond.'

She stared at him in amazement, for the moment lost
for words. She could easily have believed the man from
Harland Pharmaceuticals, with his immaculate appearance
and charming manner, to be the new locum, but not this
one. Not this man, with his scruffy appearance. The
straggly hair was worn too long, the rugged brown skin
gave the impression he spent all his life in the open, the
grey eyes looked as if they were staring at some distant
horizon and the lean, almost wolfish look suggested he
could do with a square meal.

She felt her hand clasped in a strong, dry grip while,
in growing dismay, she allowed her gaze to flicker briefly

over his clothes. The jeans were frayed around the edges and his khaki shirt, covering a T-shirt of dubious colour, had its sleeves rolled back to reveal sinewy brown arms with a covering of dark hairs, their tips turned gold by the sun.

Hastily Kate averted her eyes.

'We weren't expecting you yet. . .' she said at last, and even to herself it sounded feeble.

'So I gather. I am a few days earlier than I thought.' His voice was a lazy drawl. 'Is that a problem?'

'No. No, of course not,' Kate replied. 'I'm sorry you've been kept waiting that's all. I'm. . .I'm . . . afraid you've caught us at a rather unusual time.' She glanced at Claire. 'Is Martin around, Claire?'

The girl shook her head. 'No, he's still on his house calls.'

'I see.' Kate turned back. 'That's Martin Hogan, another partner,' she explained. 'And Richard—Dr Fleetwood, our senior partner—is at a meeting, together with our practice manager and one of the nurses. So, at the moment, I'm afraid there's only me here. . .'

'I don't have a problem with that.' The grey gaze was faintly disconcerting, and Kate found herself looking away again. Out of the corner of her eye she was vaguely aware of Gregory Sumpter, who had just finished making his appointment with Jackie and was summing up the new locum with a look of barely concealed amusement. 'Where would you like me to stack my gear?'

'Your gear?'

As Jonathan Hammond turned and looked towards the corner where he had been sitting, Kate's gaze followed his. Two huge canvas holdalls were on the floor, together with a second pair of boots. 'Oh,' she said, 'I see. Well. . .

perhaps you'd like to bring it through to the staffroom for the time being.'

Under the scrutiny of the rest of her patients—and only too aware that the two receptionists watched with open curiosity—Kate waited while he picked up his baggage, then led the way to the staffroom.

'I'm afraid,' she said as he dumped the bags in the centre of the room and looked around him, 'that I'm going to have to leave you to it for the time being. You see, I'm in the middle of surgery. You are very welcome to make yourself some tea or coffee and I'm sure there are some biscuits in the cupboard over there—'

'Paul said you'd arrange a billet,' he said interrupting her in mid-sentence.

'Billet?' She paused. 'Oh, yes, of course. I've had a word with a friend of mine who has a flat vacant. If it's all right with you, I'll take you over to see it. But I'm afraid it will have to be after I've finished surgery. Like I said, we didn't really expect you just yet.'

'No problem.' He began to prowl around the staffroom, his movements reminding Kate of a large animal—a cat. A panther, possibly or a leopard.

'Right,' she said after a moment. 'If you'll excuse me, I'll get back to my surgery. . .'

He had been staring out of the window at the car park and the hospital building next door but he swung round now. 'If you don't mind, I'll come with you,' he said.

Kate paused with one hand on the door handle, not understanding what he meant. 'Come with me?'

'Yes.' He nodded. 'Sit in with you on your surgery. You've no objection?'

She had. Every objection. The last thing she wanted was for this scruffy individual, with his casual, laid-back approach, to sit in her consulting room while she saw her patients but, caught as she was unawares, she had difficulty thinking of a refusal that wouldn't give offence. He was, after all, a doctor—a guest, really, of the practice and someone who was, in effect, helping them out. Before she could think of a suitable excuse he had joined her, crossing the room in a couple of paces.

'I find it a little claustrophobic in here,' he said, gesturing to the windows and the view of the hospital. 'I'm more used to open spaces than built-up areas.'

'Yes. Of course. You would be,' she said, suddenly helpless as the moment for excuses passed and he followed her from the room.

He seemed to tower over her as they walked down the corridor, making her feel small—fragile even. He didn't speak again and she found herself floundering desperately for something to say, anything to break the silence which, for some reason, she found disconcerting.

'I understand,' she said at last as they reached the open door of her consulting room, 'that you've been working in Africa?'

'Yep.' He nodded but offered no more information.

'Will you go back there?' She closed the door behind him, then moved a chair behind the desk, positioning it to one side of her own and indicating for him to sit down.

'Of course.' He said it as if to do anything else would be unthinkable.

'So, what did your work consist of?' She asked the question more in a bid to avoid another silence than from a desire to know.

'About the same as yours, I should say,' he said. 'The difference being that my surgery was in a bush station. A mud hut rather than a fancy, modern centre. But I doubt if the patients were any different.'

'I dare say their problems were,' Kate replied, sitting down and drawing the next set of patient records towards her.

'I wouldn't think so,' he replied. 'They were human beings I was dealing with.'

'Well, yes, of course.' Kate felt herself flush under that cool grey stare. As she pressed the buzzer she said, 'So how do you and Paul know each other?'

'Medical school.'

'I see.' She was beginning to get used to his economy with words. 'Have you been to the Isle of Wight before?'

'No. First visit.' Taking off his hat, he leaned back in the chair just as someone tapped on the door. Folding his arms, he thrust his long legs out in front of him. Tightening her lips in disapproval, Kate wondered what her patients would make of him.

'Come in,' she called.

The door opened and a woman in her thirties with a young boy came into the room.

'Ah, Janice, come in,' said Kate. 'Please take a seat. This is Mrs Goodway and her son, Damien,' she said to Jonathan Hammond. Turning to the patients again, she explained, 'Dr Hammond would like to sit in on this consultation, if you don't have any objections. If you do, however, you are perfectly within your rights to refuse—'

'Oh, we don't mind,' Janice Goodway interrupted her before she could go any further. 'We've already met, haven't we, Jon?' She grinned at Jonathan Hammond.

'Really?' Kate looked from one to the other in surprise. 'I don't understand. . .'

'In the waiting room.' It was Damien who answered, along with a cheeky grin in the locum's direction. 'It was brilliant. He was telling me all about Africa—'

'Right. Well, in that case, we'd better get on.' Suddenly Kate felt irritated, although she wasn't sure why. 'So, what seems to be the problem?'

'It's Damien,' said Janice Goodway. 'He's got this rash.'

'Let's have a look, Damien, shall we?' Kate stood up and moved round the desk until she stood in front of Damien. The boy held out his hands and immediately Kate could see the red, raised areas of the rash across the backs of his hands and between his fingers.

'We don't know what's caused it,' said Janice. 'It seems to have come on quite suddenly.'

Kate glanced up and saw to her annoyance that Janice Goodway seemed to be addressing her remarks to Jonathan Hammond rather than to herself. 'It looks like some sort of contact dermatitis,' Kate said, her voice sounding, she knew, a little more brisk than usual. 'Have you been using anything different lately?'

'How do you mean, Doctor—different? Janice turned to Kate, almost dragging her gaze away from Jonathan Hammond's lounging form.

'Well, perhaps soap or bath oil?' suggested Kate.

'No, nothing like that. . .'

'Washing powder?'

'No, Doctor. I've used the same one for years,' said Janice Goodway, then she added urgently, 'Can't you give him anything for it? It's the itching, you see. It's driving him mad. . .isn't it, Damien?' She looked down at her son.

Damien nodded.

'I can certainly give you some cream to relieve the irritation,' said Kate, 'but it's important that we identify just what it is that's causing it. Have you been touching any unusual plants in the garden, Damien?'

Damien shook his head and Janice said, 'No, Doctor, nothing like that. He's hardly been in the garden. I'm sure I don't know what it could be.'

'Well, I'll prescribe some hydrocortisone cream, which you must apply very sparingly.' Kate straightened and walked to the washbasin where she washed her hands. She returned to her desk, sat down and then, suddenly very aware of Jonathan Hammond beside her, watching, she tapped out the prescription on her computer.

'I shall want you to use this cream for a week,' she said as the prescription began to print out, 'but I still want you to go on trying to identify what is causing the dermatitis. That is important because if you don't, and you carry on having contact with whatever it is, the dermatitis will return.'

Tearing off the prescription, Kate was about to hand it to Janice when Jonathan Hammond suddenly spoke.

'Perhaps you should show Dr Chapman your model aircraft, Damien.'

'OK.' Damien turned and dived into his mother's shopping bag, pulling out a model of a Vulcan bomber.

'That's very nice, Damien,' said Kate.

'Damien made it himself,' said Jonathan Hammond.

'Good. . .'

'Yes, it is good.' The locum nodded. 'But that wasn't really the point.'

'What point?' Kate frowned, wondering what he was on about and at the same time wishing she could just get on with her surgery.

'That model-making is Damien's new hobby.'

Kate stiffened. 'You mean. . .?'

He nodded—a lazy, heavy-lidded nod, while he continued to sprawl in the chair. She suddenly had an uncontrollable and totally unreasonable urge to slap him.

'Those solvents and adhesives they use on these things are pretty potent,' he observed.

'Oh, do you really think that could be what is causing Damien's rash?' Janice Goodway was staring at Jonathan Hammond with the sort of awe that might be accredited to some great explorer or a scientist who has made some phenomenal discovery.

'Could well be.'

Kate took a deep breath. 'It's certainly worth considering,' she said coolly. 'On the other hand, it would be a shame to stop Damien's new hobby if it isn't that.'

'I don't care, really,' said Damien. 'I wasn't going to do any more anyhow. . .it got boring.'

Kate stood up, walked to the door and opened it. 'Come back if the cream doesn't give any relief,' she said.

Jonathan Hammond didn't say a word as she closed the door behind the Goodways and returned to her desk. But as she sat down, holding onto her temper with difficulty, he leaned across to look at the next set of records.

'Who's next?' he asked, reading the label. 'Robert Neville.'

'Dr Hammond.' Kate drew a deep breath. 'I don't mind you sitting in on this surgery, although I have to say it's not something I am either familiar or entirely comfortable with, but I would appreciate it if you didn't offer any contribution.'

'Oh?' He sounded innocent. 'You object to that?'

'Let's say, again it's not something I'm used to.'

'Not used to second opinions?' He seemed amazed. 'Where I've come from we work like that all the time.'

'Really? Well, it isn't something we tend to go in for here.'

'Can't think why not.' He shook his head in a mystified fashion. 'After all, if I hadn't chipped in then you wouldn't have known about the adhesives, would you? I knew because the boy showed me the plane in the waiting room.'

'It may not be the adhesives,' she replied.

He grinned. 'I bet a pound to a penny it is.'

'You may well be right, Dr Hammond—'

'Jon.'

'I'm sorry?'

'The name's Jon. I like to be called Jon. Not Dr Hammond, or Jonathan, but Jon. OK?'

'OK. Fine. Although. . .'

'Yes?' He raised his eyebrows.

'We don't usually encourage the patients to address us by our first names.'

'Fair enough.'

'You told Mrs Goodway to call you. . . Jon?'

He grinned, put his hands behind his head and leaned back even further, tilting the chair at a crazy angle. 'I did. Personally, I can't see any harm in it. . .but if that's how you do things here. . .then. . .'

'Yes, Dr Hammond, it is.'

'Jon,' he said softly.

'Very well,' she replied. To her dismay, she felt the colour touch her cheeks under his steady gaze. 'Jon.'

CHAPTER TWO

'MR NEVILLE was involved in an accident on New Year's day,' said Kate after she had been through the introductions and explanations for the second time. 'He was taken to A and E next door at the Shalbrooke, suffering from injuries to his neck and shoulders and decompression of the chest. A thoracotomy was carried out but Mr Neville is still experiencing pain and stiffness in his neck and shoulders. Isn't that so, Mr Neville?'

The patient nodded.

'How are you getting along with the ibuprofen I prescribed for you?'

'Well,' said Mr Neville ponderously, 'it helped to get rid of the pain.'

'Good.'

'But. . .' He hesitated.

'You have another problem?' asked Kate.

'Well, I seem to be getting a lot of indigestion,' he replied. 'I thought at first it was bruising from my chest injuries, but now I'm not so sure.'

'When does this indigestion come on?' asked Kate, drawing the patient's notes from his record envelope and glancing quickly through the letters from the hospital.

'About an hour after meals.'

'And when do you take the ibuprofen?'

'Oh, I always take them with a meal. You said to make sure of that, Doctor, and I always do. I say—' Mr Neville suddenly looked worried, '—you don't think it could be the tablets, causing the indigestion, do you?'

'It could well be,' Kate replied. 'It does happen sometimes.'

'Oh, dear.' Mr Neville looked more concerned than ever. 'Does that mean I should stop taking them?'

'I was about to suggest that,' Kate replied.

At that moment Jonathan Hammond shifted slightly in his chair, and once again she was suddenly, almost overwhelmingly aware of his presence in the room. And once again she found herself wishing she hadn't agreed to let him stay. He hadn't interrupted as he had with Damien Goodway, but this time, if anything, his silence was somehow worse, as if he was waiting to see what she would do—testing her in some way.

'But they were working,' Mr Neville protested. 'My neck and shoulders were really beginning to feel better. If I stop taking the tablets now I might be back at square one. It was a real clout I had, you know.' He looked at Jon Hammond as he spoke, including him in the conversation.

'It must have been.' There was just the right degree of sympathy in Jon Hammond's reply to encourage further confidences.

'My car was practically a write-off. . .'

'Really? What exactly did you hit?'

'I didn't hit anything. It hit me!' There was indignation in Mr Neville's voice now, outrage even.

'He must have been travelling,' observed Jon Hammond.

'He was. . .'

At that point Kate intervened. 'What I think we'll do,' she said firmly, 'is to take you off the ibuprofen and—'

'So, what was it?' Jon Hammond carried on talking.

'A ruddy milk float, that's what!' Mr Neville was positively bristling with indignation.

'Get away.'

'Take you off the ibuprofen,' Kate repeated firmly, 'and try a soluble paracetamol-based drug.' She didn't dare look at Jon Hammond. 'That,' she went on hurriedly, 'should still help to control the pain for you but it will be a lot more gentle on the stomach lining. If that doesn't do the trick, and you still get pain, I think we need to consider some further physiotherapy.'

Quickly she tapped in a prescription, and waited for it to print while Mr Neville continued to give Jon Hammond further details of his accident. At last she tore off the form and, standing up, handed it across the desk.

'There you are,' she said.

'Thank you. Thank you very much, Dr Chapman. And you.' Mr Neville nodded towards the locum. 'Thank you as well. Very good of you to see me. I always did say two heads are better than one.'

As Mr Neville left the room, shutting the door behind him, Jon Hammond gave a low chuckle.

'I'm glad you find all this so funny,' said Kate, sinking back into her chair again, but there was no irritation in her voice now.

'It wasn't that I particularly found anything funny,' he replied, 'it's just what we were saying before about people's problems being the same. They're just more relevant to wherever they happen to be. Your Mr Neville reminded me of a patient I once saw on the bush station. He, too, had been involved in a collision...only in his case it had been with a buffalo.'

Kate found herself smiling, and after a moment she

threw him a sideways glance. 'What area do you work in?' she asked.

'I've been all over Africa,' he said. 'Ethiopia, Biafra, Nigeria—but more recently I've been in Tanzania.'

'You obviously enjoy that type of life.'

'Let's say it would take a lot to make me give it up.' He paused and glanced round Kate's consulting room— at the medical cabinets and chest, the bookshelves, the brightly patterned curtains around the examination cubicle, the comfortable chairs. 'You seem to have a nice little set-up for yourself here.'

Kate shrugged. 'I like it,' she said.

'So, what are you, exactly, in the pecking order?'

'Junior partner, I'm afraid.'

He shrugged. 'Things change.'

'Not much chance of that around here.' Kate gave a short laugh. 'The senior partner is only in his early forties. I shouldn't think he's got too many thoughts of retiring just yet, especially as he has two children to bring up— single-handed as well.'

'That's Richard Fleetwood?' asked Jon, and when Kate nodded, he said, 'Is he divorced?'

'No, widowed, actually. His wife died of leukaemia three years ago.'

'Tragic.'

'Yes. It was. Very.'

'So, who else is there? Apart from Paul.'

'Martin. Martin Hogan. He, too, is a family man— three children.'

'But presumably a wife in evidence as well.'

'Very much so.' Kate paused and allowed herself a brief smile. 'Yes, Patsy is very much in evidence. You'll meet her in due course. You'll meet all of them.'

'Who is this friend of yours? The one with the vacant flat.'

'Oh, that's Helen. Helen Turner.'

'Does she work here as well?'

'No, she works at the hospital next door. . .'

'The Shalbrooke?'

'Yes, she's Senior Sister on Accident and Emergency.'

'No doubt she had the pleasure of removing the glass from your Mr Neville's posterier on New Year's Day.'

Kate laughed. 'No doubt she did. Now, that's enough of these trivialities. I'll fill you in on everyone else later but now I really must get on with this surgery.'

Somehow, unbelievably, the mood had lightened, the tension lifted, and Kate got through the rest of the surgery without further incident.

It was getting late by the time she had introduced Jon Hammond to Martin Hogan and then to Richard Fleetwood and Elizabeth French, the practice manager, when they returned from their meeting.

'It's good to have you aboard,' said Richard. 'Paul told us you're recovering from some tropical virus. You'll have to say if you find the workload too much.'

'I dare say I'll cope,' Jon replied.

'Even so. You mustn't overdo things. These viruses can take their toll. What was it exactly?'

'No one really knew. One of those things without a name. But you're right.' He nodded. 'It was pretty deadly. Not something I'd want to go through again.'

A little later, after stowing Jon's gear in the boot of Kate's car, they left the Fleetwood Centre.

'You're right about Richard Fleetwood being young to be a senior partner,' Jon observed as they left the village of Shalbrooke behind and joined the traffic on the main road. 'Was he the founder of the place?'

'No.' Kate shook her head. 'That was his father, Leo. He's in his seventies now. Retired of course. Fills his days with golf and sailing.'

'Does he help out at the centre?'

'Not if Richard can help it,' she replied, pulling a wry expression.

'I see.'

They drove in silence for a while as they headed inland. Kate suddenly became aware that he was watching her. Taking her eyes briefly from the road, she threw him a glance.

'I was just thinking,' he said. 'I now know about practically every member of staff at the Fleetwood Centre, except for you.'

'Me?'

'Yes, you've told me nothing about yourself.'

She shrugged. 'What exactly do you want to know?'

'Well, for a start, you've filled me in on everyone else's marital status.'

'Oh, I'm not married,' she said quickly.

'I didn't for one moment think you were.'

'Oh.' Momentarily she was taken aback and didn't know what to say. There was something in the way he had spoken that left her feeling indignant. 'I hadn't realised it was that obvious,' she said.

'Maybe it isn't—to some,' he replied.

'But you? You knew?' Her tone was sarcastic.

'Yes. I knew. . .or rather I guessed.'

Kate swallowed, forcing herself not to bite back but to concentrate instead on negotiating the twists and turns in the country lanes. When he remained silent she said, 'What about you?'

'Me?' The reply was lazy. 'What about me?'

'Are you married?'

'No.' Another silence followed the single monosyllable, then he added, 'I doubt anyone would have me.'

'No,' Kate replied wryly. 'I doubt they would.'

He didn't answer and suddenly she felt a stab of guilt that she might have somehow overstepped the mark. 'What I meant,' she said, throwing him another quick glance, 'was that most women would find your lifestyle. . .well, difficult to cope with.'

'Don't worry,' he replied shortly. 'I know exactly what you meant.'

Kate bit her lip but refrained from further comment, afraid she would simply dig an even bigger hole for herself.

'I dare say,' he said after a moment, 'that what you say is true—that a woman might well have difficulty accepting my lifestyle—but, likewise, I have to say I've never yet found the woman I would want to spend the rest of my life with.'

There seemed a slightly derisive note in his voice and Kate found herself refraining from commenting further, instead concentrating even more on her driving while Jon looked out of the window at the surrounding countryside.

'What's the castle?' he asked after a while, craning his neck to look over his shoulder.

'That's Carisbrooke,' Kate replied, nodding towards the castle of grey stone—its battlements dramatically etched against a sky of pale viridian. 'King Charles I was imprisoned there before his execution.'

Jon turned sideways for a better look. 'Pretty impressive sort of place,' he said after a moment. 'Norman, is it?'

Kate nodded and then, as the road dipped and they

followed a sign for Gatcombe, she said, 'Where is your home? When you are in this country, I mean?'

'I don't really have a base here any more,' he replied. 'It seemed senseless keeping a flat on when I spent so little time here. My mother lives near Newbury,' he added, as if as an afterthought.

'Is that where you've been convalescing?'

'No. I've been staying with some VSO friends in Norfolk.'

He offered no further information and Kate was left with an even stronger impression of a drifter. Someone with no roots, little family. No ties, no responsibilities. He'd mentioned his mother but hadn't seemed to want to elaborate. She wondered if they'd fallen out or maybe just lost touch.

She was forced to dismiss her speculations as they reached Gatcombe and she drove into the lane where Helen Turner lived with her father in what had once been the Turner family home.

It was almost dusk and as Kate parked the car on the gravel drive and they climbed out they were greeted by the smell of woodsmoke fires and an enthusiastic welcome from an elderly red setter who ambled up to the car to meet them.

'Hello, Chester, old boy.' Kate bent over to fondle the dog's greying muzzle and his soft, silky ears.

The house was old. Built of Island stone, it had once been the coachman's house, part of the estate of a nearby manor. Its roof of slate tiles was gabled while ivy covered its walls, twisting around the sash windows and trailing across the front entrance. To the left of the house stood the coach-house and the stables, with the hayloft above having been converted in recent years into an attractive flat.

'Kate. We've been expecting you.' Helen suddenly appeared in the doorway of the house. She had changed out of her sister's uniform into a warm sweater, which she wore over a long, floral skirt. Kate, in the rather severe suit she was wearing, suddenly felt decidedly overdressed alongside Helen, so charmingly relaxed, and Jon, so casual and laid-back it looked as if it might take an earthquake to galvanise him into action.

'Sorry we're late, Helen,' she said. 'Surgery went on even longer than I feared it might. But we finally got here. Helen, this is Jonathan Hammond. Jon,. . .' she turned as he loped round the car '. . .this is Helen Turner.'

'Hi, there.' He took her outstretched hand and Kate— who was watching Helen to see her reaction—saw her eyes widen slightly in surprise. No doubt she had been expecting the immaculate Gregory Sumpter whom she had seen in Reception, not this scruffy character. Kate hoped she wouldn't change her mind about letting him rent the flat. 'Didn't I see you earlier at the centre?' he added before Kate had the chance to say anything further.

'Well, I was there. . .yes.' Helen paused. 'But I don't think I saw you.'

'No. You probably didn't.' He grinned. 'But I saw you. It isn't often I miss a pretty lady.'

Helen laughed. It was her usual, easy, friendly laugh but Kate felt a sudden unreasonable rush of irritation again. What was it about this man that made her feel like that?

'Well, it's nice to meet you, Dr Hammond,' Helen said as she led the way into the house. 'Welcome to the Isle of Wight. Kate tells me you are to be locum for Paul

Wooldridge for a time. I hope you'll be happy here with us all. We're a close community, but I'm sure you'll find everyone very friendly.'

Kate suddenly felt guilty. Helen had just said all the things she should have said. Had she said them? Had she welcomed him, or had she been so taken aback by his appearance and irritated by his attitude that she had completely forgotten her manners? Feeling slightly subdued, and while the locum was telling Helen to call him Jon, she followed them through the hall into a cosy sitting room at the back of the house.

Harry Turner, Helen's father, was sitting in a leather armchair, apparently watching television. He didn't look round as they came into the room.

'Dad.' Helen leaned over the chair and touched his arm. 'Look who's come to see you. It's Kate—Dr Chapman— and she's brought a friend with her.'

A startled expression on his face, Harry Turner looked round.

Kate moved forward into his line of vision. 'Hello, Harry,' she said. 'How are you today?'

'Are you Margaret Thatcher?' Harry tried to stand up.

'No, Dad,' said Helen patiently. 'This is Kate. Kate Chapman.'

'And who are you?' Harry glared at Jon Hammond, who hovered in the doorway. Not giving anyone a chance to reply, he went on, 'I don't know how you've got the nerve to show your face in this house, not after what you did to the family.'

'Dad,' said Helen gently, gripping his shoulder to restrain him, 'it's not Ralph, it's Dr Hammond. He's the new locum at the Fleetwood Centre. He's from Africa—

isn't that so?' She raised her eyebrows at Jon who nodded in reply.

'Africa? I said there would be trouble there,' Harry went on. 'Have they put Mandela in prison?'

Helen straightened and gave a helpless little shrug. 'Sorry about this,' she murmured.

'Don't worry about it,' Kate replied. 'Tell you what, why don't you leave Harry and me to have a little chat while you show Jon the flat?'

'Yes, all right.' Helen seemed relieved by the suggestion and—indicating for Jon to follow her—she went out of the sitting room, leaving Kate alone with Harry.

Harry had returned to watching television and had apparently forgotten Kate's presence in the room. Carefully, so as not to disturb him further, she sat down on the sofa alongside his armchair. Harry had been her patient for a long time and in growing frustration she had watched Alzheimer's disease claim him and reduce him to a mere shadow of his former self.

It was hard to believe that the man before her had not only once been the senior partner in a firm of solicitors but had also been a first-class sailor. He had also had the reputation of being something of a demon on the tennis court, and had retained his upright posture and fine physical form for so long that it was easy to forget what was happening to his brain. More recently, however, he had developed a stoop, and as the disease had taken its dreadful toll he had lost weight and also, it would seem, that spark of determination which had once been so characteristic of him.

Helen was nursing him to the best of her ability, together with the help of the day centre at the Shalbrooke, but Kate feared the day was approaching even more rapidly than Helen realised when Harry would need full-time care.

Even as she watched him, agonising over the loss of such a fine personality, he turned his head and looked at her.

'Why, Kate,' he said. 'Where did you spring from? How lovely to see you.'

It was the old Harry. The one they all knew and loved so much. Kate swallowed. 'Hello, Harry,' she said gently.

'Does Helen know you're here?'

'Yes, she does. She's showing a colleague of mine round the stable flat. He may be renting it for a while.'

'What a splendid idea. Did you know Siobhan's coming here in the summer?'

'Yes, Harry, Helen did say,' Kate replied.

'That's my niece's girl, you know,' he said, then added proudly, 'She's training for the paramedics. I'm so pleased because she was such a little scrap of a thing when she was born. They didn't think she'd survive. . .'

'It just goes to show, doesn't it?' Kate blinked. Somehow Harry's lucid moments were even harder to bear than those other times.

'How are you feeling, Harry?' she said after a moment.

'Not too bad, really,' he said. 'Mustn't grumble—there are a lot worse off than me.'

'Are you eating well?'

'If I'm honest, I don't enjoy my food any more—but, then, there are a lot of things I don't enjoy any more.'

'What sort of things, Harry?' Kate asked with a smile.

He stared at her for a long moment, and just as they heard the sounds of Helen and Jon returning he shook his head slightly. 'You know something?' he said. 'I'm blessed if I can remember.'

She leaned forward and briefly covered his hand with her own, at the same time turning her head to look up at the other two who by that time had come back into the room.

'Well,' said Helen with a quick, apprehensive look at her father, almost as if she wondered what he had been saying to Kate or was dreading what he might be about to say next, 'Jon likes the flat.'

'Good.' Kate stood up. 'So when can he move in?'

'I should think the painters will be through in the next couple of days,' Helen replied, 'so certainly by the weekend.' She paused and looked from Jon to Kate, then back to Jon again. 'But what will you do in the meantime?'

Jon shrugged but before he could answer Kate said, 'I thought I'd take him to the Thistle and Rose. I'm sure Lily will have a room for him just until the weekend—that's the local at Shalbrooke, if that's OK?' She raised her eyebrows and Jon nodded.

'That sounds fine. I'm not fussy. I can doss down anywhere.'

'I think we can be a little more positive than that,' Kate replied crisply, and was aware of Helen's slightly surprised look. 'I think, however, we should be going now. Thanks, Helen, for everything. Goodbye, Harry.' She leaned over to look at him, but Harry was watching television again and didn't answer.

'Dad,' said Helen, 'Kate's just going.'

'Who?' Harry looked up but the expression in his eyes was blank again as he looked at Kate.

'Kate,' said Helen, and there was a very slight edge of exasperation in her voice that wasn't lost on Kate or, Kate suspected, on Jon Hammond.

'Who's she?' demanded Harry indignantly. 'What's she

doing here?' She should be at Westminster. The house is sitting tonight.'

They went, leaving Harry in his own lost world.

'It's a devastating disease,' said Jon as they drove away from the Coach House.

Kate nodded. 'More so in this case if you'd known Harry before.'

'They are friends of yours?'

'Yes, Helen and I were at school together—back in the seventies.'

'And she isn't married either?'

'No.' Kate paused, and for some unknown reason found herself volunteering further information. 'I live in hopes that she and Richard Fleetwood will eventually get together.'

'Is that a possibility?' He sounded interested.

'They are very fond of each other. . .'

'You say he's widowed?'

'Yes, his wife, Diana, was also a friend of ours. In fact, she, Helen and I were inseparable at one time.'

'You weren't joking, were you, when you said this was a close community?'

'It's inevitable, living on an island,' Kate retorted, immediately on the defensive.

He didn't reply. After a while he said, 'So, where do you live?'

'At Cowes. I have an apartment on the seafront.'

'Ah!' he said knowingly, and although he offered no further comment he left Kate feeling vaguely uneasy, wondering what he had meant.

They were silent after that as they drove back to the village of Shalbrooke, where Kate brought the car to a halt on the forecourt of the Thistle and Rose pub.

'We'll see if we can fix up a few nights' accommodation for you here,' she said as she switched off the engine.

'Do they do food as well?' he asked, peering up at the brightly lit front façade of the building.

Kate felt another stab of guilt. He must be hungry and he'd not really been offered anything to eat since he had arrived. 'Lily's meals are the pride of the Wight,' she said.

'Good,' he replied, confirming her suspicions by adding, 'I'm starving.'

As they walked across the car park in the chill of the March evening he said, 'You haven't eaten either—will you join me?'

'Well. . .' she searched for an excuse '. . .I really should be getting home. . .'

'Oh, come on. Surely you're not going to make me eat alone on my first night here. What happened to all this friendly Island hospitality I've been hearing about?'

Kate flushed in spite of the teasing note in his voice. 'Very well,' she said tightly, 'but I mustn't be too long.'

To Kate's surprise, the pub was crowded. She hadn't expected that for mid-week in March. They ordered drinks and the day's 'special', which turned out to be chicken and mushroom pie. While Jon carried their drinks to the one empty table in the far corner of the bar Kate made inquiries about accommodation, and found to her dismay the reason for the unusual amount of activity.

'Their rooms are fully booked,' she said as she joined Jon and sat down beside him. 'Apparently, these people are cyclists, taking part in a round the Island race at the weekend.'

'Not to worry.' He took a mouthful of his beer and gave a deep sigh of satisfaction.

'You don't understand,' said Kate. 'The story's likely

to be the same wherever we go. and. . .' she glanced at
her watch '. . .it's getting late.'

Still he didn't seem worried. He finished his beer, and
when their food arrived he tucked in as if it was the first
food he'd had for a week. Kate, watching, found herself
wondering if that wasn't the case. Which was ridiculous,
really, she told herself. He'd been staying with friends.
Wasn't that what he'd said? They surely would have fed
him. And even if they hadn't, he couldn't be hard up. She
wasn't sure what he would be paid for his work in Africa
but he was, after all, a doctor.

Her gaze moved from his unkempt fair hair to the
shadow on his jaw, then down to the frayed jeans and
crumpled shirt.

Had she misjudged him?

Uneasily she shifted in her seat, suddenly finding difficulty in swallowing her food—which was surprising
because it was as delicious as Lily's food always was. In
sudden desperation she wondered what she was going to
do with him. Maybe, she thought, she should phone
Richard and see whether he could put him up for the
night. Then she remembered that Richard had relatives
staying with him at his house at Newtown Creek.

Jon finished eating, then with another loud sigh put
down his knife and fork and leaned back in his chair.
'That's better,' he said. 'I feel more human now. Ready
to face whatever it is I have to face.' He winked at her.

'What do you mean?' She frowned.

'My night on the beach.'

'On the beach!' she exclaimed, her eyes widening.
'What are you talking about?'

'Well, it looks like that may be my only option. Does
Cowes have a pier?'

'Don't be silly,' she said, and because she was worried it came out more sharply than she'd intended.

'Oh, I'm quite used to it,' he said nonchalantly. 'Sleeping rough, I mean. I do it all the time in Africa.'

'I would say there's a bit of difference between sleeping in the open in Africa and sleeping on the beach in England on a cold night in March,' she retorted.

'Don't you believe it,' he replied darkly. 'African nights can get very chilly.'

'Even so,' she snapped, 'I can't allow it. Whatever would the other partners think if they heard their locum was sleeping on the beach like some...some vagrant.'

He was silent for a moment and then, his steady gaze meeting hers, he said softly, 'So what do you suggest?'

She stared at him in silent exasperation. At last she said, 'I suppose you'd better come home with me.'

'With you?' His eyes widened but she couldn't fail to see the amusement in them.

'That's what I said.'

'You mean you have room in this apartment of yours on the seafront at Cowes?'

He was mocking her now and she knew it. 'It's a two-bedroomed apartment,' she said tightly, pushing her plate away, her meal only half-eaten, as she got to her feet.

'I didn't for one moment imagine it was anything else,' he said solemnly. 'I somehow couldn't believe, on such short acquaintance, you would be inviting me to share your bed.'

CHAPTER THREE

KATE had chosen to ignore Jon's remark, but as she parked her car in the garage behind the apartment block where she lived she was aware of a growing sense of unease. It was quite dark by now but the close proximity of the sea was almost tangible in the freshness of the air, the low roar of the surf and the taste of salt.

Jon Hammond dragged his luggage from the boot of her car, then paused and looked around, his head thrown back as he took in great lungfuls of the heady air while Kate unlocked the ground-floor door of her apartment and flicked the light switch. As the narrow hallway was suffused with sudden light he turned and looked at her.

'The sea sounds wild,' he said, stepping into the hall and moving to one side so that Kate could close the door.

'It often is at this time of the year. Something to do with spring tides,' she said, squeezing past him and leading the way up the stairs. 'My apartment is up here,' she explained. 'There are six altogether, three on the ground floor and three upstairs.'

'How long have you been here?' he asked as they reached the landing.

'Five years,' she replied. 'I moved in soon after they were built—when I joined the practice.'

'Where were you before that?'

'London,' she said abruptly.

'You do leave your Island sometimes, then?' The mocking note was back in his voice, only this time it seemed more teasing than mocking.

'Sometimes it's unavoidable when it comes to things like training...and jobs,' she replied shortly. Inserting the key in the door, she pushed it open. 'I was extremely lucky to get the partnership,' she added.

'If you hadn't, would you have stayed in London?'

'No.' It came out sharply and as she switched on the lights she was aware of his look of surprise. 'I. . .I didn't like London very much. I certainly wouldn't have wanted to return there.'

She hurried forward and dumped her case and her shoulder-bag. She drew the blinds across the picture window, shutting out the night sky, the street lights on the sea front and the crashing surf as it broke on the shingle and hit the seawall.

'You can bring your bags in here,' she went on as she walked out of the sitting room into a wide passage and opened a door. 'The bed is made up and the bathroom is there.' She pointed to another closed door. 'I'll leave you to sort yourself out. Would you like some coffee?'

'He nodded. 'That would be nice. Thanks.'

Suddenly Kate found she couldn't meet his gaze. Embarrassed, she hurried back through the sitting room to the kitchen, where she filled the jug kettle and plugged it in.

Moments later, after she'd spooned fresh coffee into the cafetière and poured on boiling water, she heard the toilet flush and then the sound of running water in the bathroom. Ordinary, everyday sounds that simply signified the presence of another human being, but to Kate it felt strange. It was some time since she'd had anyone to stay and when she did it was usually a relative or an old schoolfriend. . .another female. It was a very long time since she'd had a man around. Her hand shook slightly as she finished pouring the water.

In fact, there hadn't been anyone since Alistair.

She mustn't think of him now, she told herself desperately. Already she could feel the first stirring of panic deep inside. She shouldn't have asked Jon Hammond to come here. It was a mistake. She knew that. It had been foolish, but she only had herself to blame. She should have phoned Richard or Martin when the pub was full and explained the situation. One of them would have come up with some solution. They wouldn't have expected her to bring him back here. . .

'Can I help?'

She jumped violently and spun round, knocking over the carton of milk she'd just taken out of the fridge. He was standing behind her.

'Oh,' she gasped, 'I didn't know you were there. . . didn't hear you. . .I thought you were still in the bedroom.'

'Hey, steady on. I didn't mean to startle you.' He backed away slightly, obviously amazed at her reaction.

'It's OK. . . It's all right.' Frantically she picked up the carton, then grabbed a cloth and began mopping up the spilt milk. When she had finished, only too aware that he was still watching her curiously, she turned to pick up the tray which she'd set with the cafetière, two mugs, sugar, milk and a plate of digestive biscuits.

'Here,' he said, stepping forward, 'let me take that.' Helplessly she let him, powerless for the moment to protest.

She followed him into the sitting room and sank onto the sofa whilst he set down the tray on her large coffee-table, before sitting down himself in one of the cane-backed armchairs.

He instantly looked at home, drawing up one ankle, gripping it and resting it on his knee while he gazed round her room at the decor, her treasures, her belongings—everything that made up her life and at the same time gave away her tastes and her personality. The brief respite also gave her space to recover from the sudden attack of nerves.

Eventually she was able to lean forward and pour the coffee, indicating for him to help himself to milk, sugar and biscuits. Then, with a little sigh, she leaned back, curled her hands around her mug and sipped the hot, infinitely comforting contents.

They spoke little and Kate found herself wondering just what he would think if he knew exactly why she had jumped so violently. Not that he would guess, of course. No one would. Not in a million years would anyone guess. And if they did they wouldn't believe it.

'Are you coming into the centre tomorrow?' she asked at last, hoping he would say no. The last thing she wanted was to have him sitting in on her surgeries again.

To her relief he shook his head. 'No,' he said, 'I've agreed with Richard Fleetwood that I don't start surgeries until next week, as we arranged. I have a few things to do before then.' He gave a wry chuckle. 'Like getting a haircut and buying some new clothes.'

Thank God for that, thought Kate, briefly allowing her gaze to fall on his tatty jeans and the hole in the sole of his trainers which had replaced his boots. To a certain extent she could understand his casual form of dress if he had only recently returned from the bush, but she had feared that he had not intended doing anything about it before he started taking surgeries. 'I'll point you in the direction of the shops,' she said.

'Thanks. I guess I'll also need to arrange for some sort of transport.'

'There's a spare car at the centre,' she said quickly. 'Your predecessor, Simon Phillips, used it. We keep it for emergencies—if anyone's car is off the road, that sort of thing. In fact, Elizabeth French is using it at the moment as her car is being repaired. I expect Richard forgot to mention it, but, you're quite right, you will need transport, not only to get between Shalbrooke and Gatcombe but for house calls.'

'Talking of house calls,' he said, 'I was thinking it might be a good idea for the next couple of days if I were to accompany you on yours. Just to familiarise myself with the locality.'

She wanted to refuse. The last thing she wanted was to have him in tow, especially if his presence was going to be anything like it had been in her consulting room. But somehow she couldn't quite bring herself to say no. It would, she knew, sound petty and childish, and the last thing she wanted was for him to think either of those things of her. Instead, she stood up, neither granting nor refusing his request. 'I must be getting to bed,' she said. 'I usually make an early start in the mornings.'

He looked a bit startled at her abruptness, then he drained his mug before he, too, rose. 'I think I'll join you.' He grinned. 'Figuratively speaking, of course.'

'Quite. Well, goodnight, then,' she said stiffly, awkwardly.

'Goodnight.' He paused. 'Oh, and Kate?' She had turned away but she stopped.

'Yes?' she said, without turning round.

'Thanks,' he said. 'Thanks for everything today, and for letting me stay. It must be putting you out, but I do appreciate it.'

'That's OK,' she heard herself say. 'You're not really putting me out. . .'

'But you aren't used to it, are you?'

'What?' She felt herself stiffen.

'Having someone to stay.'

'No. No, I suppose I'm not. . .'

'I can understand that,' he said quietly. 'I'm a bit of a loner myself.'

'Yes, well. . .'

'I'll try not to disrupt you more than I can help.'

'Thank you,' she replied. 'Goodnight. . . Jon.'

'Goodnight, Kate.'

She sat on her bed, wondering what on earth she had done. She didn't know this man from Adam. He had turned up at the centre looking like a tramp. He had cajoled her into letting him sit in on her surgery and shamed her into sharing a meal with him. His earlier, light-hearted quip about her invitation not including sharing her bed had set her nerves on edge. And, really, it was against her better judgement that he was spending the night in her spare room.

At least. . .she hoped he was in the spare room. She hadn't actually heard him go into the bedroom. He had still been in the sitting room when she had left him. She lifted her head and listened, straining her ears, but there was only silence in the flat, and beyond—outside—the muted roar of the sea.

In his favour, of course, was the fact that he was a doctor, a professional man. Alistair had also been a professional man—a lawyer, a little voice niggled at the back of Kate's mind.

But Jonathan Hammond was a friend of Paul's. That, however, had been a long time ago. By his own admission, he hadn't seen Paul for years. Anything could have happened to him in those interim years.

She knew he'd been ill—a virus, he'd said. But supposing it hadn't been a virus. Supposing he'd lied. Supposing he'd been suffering from some sort of psychotic illness that left him not responsible for his actions. What if he had planned the whole thing and even now was waiting for the right moment to pounce?

Pounce was a good word, she thought irrelevently. He had reminded her of some large cat in his movements— lithe, panther-like. . .

She shifted uneasily and picked up her hairbrush, staring at it and judging its effectiveness as a weapon should the need arise.

She had been a fool to allow him here. She knew that. She should have known better, especially after her own experience. Because if life had taught Kate one thing it was that you can never take someone at face value. That, even when you think you know someone well, there is always something you don't know, some dark side just waiting to erupt into the light.

She shivered, a sudden, violent shiver. The sort of shiver that her grandmother had always referred to as someone walking on one's grave.

Standing up, she crossed swiftly to the door and turned the key. Then, for good measure, she took the chair from the corner of her room and wedged the back under the doorhandle.

It took her a long time to get to sleep and when she

did her dreams were troubled—the sort of dreams that had haunted her when she had first returned from London. The dreams that had abated recently.

She must have slept because the next thing she knew pale sunshine filled the room. She lay still for a few moments, listening to the sea, and gradually became aware that she could hear another sound—again of water but this time of rushing water, as if someone was using the shower. Turning her head, she glanced at the clock on her bedside table. Five-thirty. Her house guest was obviously an early riser.

In the clear, early sunlight her fears of the night before seemed remote, ludicrous even. With a sigh, she sat up and swung her legs out of bed to the floor. She stood up then padded silently to the window and, flinging back the curtains, stared out.

The sea was quieter than it had been the night before. No longer did it crash and foam against the sea wall. Now, although the waves were still white-capped, it seemed to lie at rest, like some great army gathering its resources for another onslaught. In the distance the mainland coastline, partly shrouded in mist, looked remote, as if it belonged to some other world.

She turned from the window and struggled into her bathrobe. Tying the belt tightly, she took a deep breath. Crossing the room, she removed the chair, unlocked and opened the door then peered cautiously out.

All was silent now. She didn't know whether Jon was still in the bathroom or not. The door was tightly shut but there was no sound from within. Silently crossing the passage, she stopped at the bathroom door, bent her head and listened intently.

'It's OK. You can go in.'

Her head shot up and she saw him standing in the sitting-room doorway.

'I had an early shower,' he said, 'so I'd be out of your way.'

'Oh, I see.' For a moment she was lost for words. Feeling decidedly uncomfortable, she said, 'Did you sleep well?'

'Pretty well, thanks. And you?'

'Er. . .yes, not too badly.' She stared at him. His hair, wet and slicked back from his face, accentuated his strong bone structure. He wore the frayed jeans again but a different T-shirt—a dark green one that looked as if it had shrunk at some time and was too tight for him across the chest and shoulders. His feet were bare and for some inexplicable reason it made him appear vulnerable and her to feel suddenly protective towards him.

'I must get on,' she muttered, averting her eyes. 'Er. . . help yourself to tea. . .coffee,. . .toast. . .whatever. . .' She trailed off and bolted into the bathroom, snapping the door shut behind her and turning the key.

After she'd showered and dressed she found him in the sitting room at the window with a mug of tea in his hands, staring out across the sea. He turned as he heard her come into the room.

'Wonderful view you have,' he said admiringly.

'Yes,' she agreed, 'it is pretty special. It's a very coveted position here, especially during Cowes Week.'

'Do you sail?' he asked, turning back to the view.

'Sometimes. The practice has its own yacht—*Mistral*,' she said.

'Is that so?' He threw her a quick look.

'How about you?'

He shook his head. 'Never had the opportunity, but it's something that appeals.'

'We shall be taking the boat from its winter mooring soon. You'll have to get Richard to take you out. He's a very experienced yachtsman.' She turned away from the window as she spoke.

'I've made you toast and boiled the kettle,' he said, 'but I didn't know whether you drank tea or coffee in the morning.'

'Oh, coffee. . . Thank you,' she said, following him into the kitchen. She hadn't the heart to tell him she rarely ate an early breakfast, preferring instead to take a break just before surgery after she'd dealt with the morning's post.

Somehow, with the help of a glass of fruit juice and two cups of coffee, she managed to wash down one slice of toast spread with orange marmalade.

'I think,' she said when she had finished, 'you'd better let me drive you into town.'

He nodded. 'Thanks, then I'll take myself off to do my shopping.' He glanced down at his clothes. 'I can hardly take surgery in these.'

Silently she agreed. What had been acceptable in the Tanzanian bush probably wouldn't go down so well with the predominantly retired population of the Island.

It was almost with a sense of relief that a little later Kate dropped him off in town and saw the tall rangy form lope away through the crowd of early morning shoppers. With a little sigh she drove to Shalbrooke, parked her car in the Fleetwood Centre car park and thankfully took herself off to the comparative solitude of her consulting room.

She was about halfway through her pile of morning mail when Elizabeth French suddenly looked round the door.

'Hello, Kate,' she smiled. 'All well?'

'I think so.' Kate sighed.

'What do you think of him?'

'Who?' asked Kate, knowing full well to whom she was referring.

'Crocodile Dundee.'

'Who. . .?'

Elizabeth laughed. 'That's what the girls in Reception have nicknamed him. I must say he certainly looks a character. Maybe he'll brighten the place up a bit.'

'Yes, maybe he will,' said Kate.

'You don't sound so sure.'

'I guess I just hadn't bargained on having him as a house guest, that's all,' said Kate wearily.

'House guest?' Elizabeth stared at her. 'Whatever do you mean? I understood from Richard that he was going to be staying in Helen Turner's flat.'

'Oh, he is. . .eventually,' said Kate. 'But Helen has the painters in and the flat apparently isn't quite ready. . .so in a wild moment I agreed that he could stay with me for a few days.'

'Couldn't we have booked him in somewhere. . .?'

'I tried but. . .oh, it's a long story. Let's just say it looks like I'm lumbered for the moment.'

'He's not a problem for you, Kate, is he?' Elizabeth suddenly looked concerned. 'Because if he is I'm sure we can—'

'No,' she interrupted, 'he's not a problem. Actually, he's no trouble at all. And, let's face it, it's only for one or two more nights at the most.'

'Well, if you're sure. He's not starting surgeries until next week, is he?'

'No, but he wants to come out on house calls with me—

to familiarise himself with the neighbourhood,' she added.

'Well, that seems a sensible idea,' said Elizabeth.

'Yes, I suppose it is,' Kate heard herself saying.

And so it was, she thought as Elizabeth left the room and went back to her office. So, if that was the case, why as the morning wore on did she find herself anticipating her house calls with a sense of dread? At least, she assumed it was dread she felt. She couldn't think of another word to adequately describe the feeling that flooded over her every time she thought of it. It felt a bit like excitement but it couldn't possibly be that so it had to be dread.

She found him in reception after she'd finished morning surgery. He appeared to be chatting up the receptionists, Claire and Jackie, who—if their rapt expressions were anything to go by—were hanging on his every word. As Kate walked round the desk and into the office area she realised that the conversation centred on Jon Hammond's life in Tanzania.

He looked up as she came in, his calm grey, gaze meeting hers.

'Hi,' he said softly. 'Good morning?'

'Yes,' she replied, aware of some intimacy in his manner. An intimacy born, no doubt, from the shared circumstances of the past twenty-four hours, but an intimacy, nevertheless, that Kate didn't want to encourage. 'Yes, not too bad, thanks. Do you still want to come on house calls with me?' It came out rather sharply and she saw a slight frown crease his forehead.

'Why, yes,' he said. 'Yes, of course.' He had been sitting in one corner of the office, alongside the massive filing cabinets that housed patient records, but he got to his feet now.

'Dr Hammond was telling us all about life on safari,' breathed Claire. 'He's seen it all—elephant herds at dawn around a waterhole, thousands of flamingoes in flight, a charging rhino and those vasts herds of wildebeest on the run—just like you see in those wildlife programmes on the telly.'

'Has he now?' said Kate coolly.

'But I expect he's told you all that,' said Jackie, 'seeing that he's staying with you.'

Kate threw the girl a sharp glance but there was a look of innocence on her face. It didn't, however, fool Kate for one moment. She knew the girls would really make a meal of the fact that Jon Hammond was her house guest. Choosing to ignore the remark, she walked across the office and picked up the list and records for her house calls.

With a wave to the girls, Jon joined her and together they walked out of the centre into the car park. It was a bright day but there was a chilly March wind that rippled through the daffodils in the flower-beds and chased white wisps of cloud across the blue of the sky. Kate noticed that although Jon still wore the frayed jeans and green T-shirt he was also wearing a denim jacket.

'I dare say you find it cold here,' she said as she unlocked her car. 'After Africa, I mean.'

'You could say that.' He grinned as he climbed into the car. 'Mind you, that's not the only thing I find different. Take seat belts, for example. Where I was, I doubt they'd even heard of them.' He fastened his as he spoke. Glancing at Kate as she started the car, he said, 'So, what do you have this morning?'

'New baby,' she replied, reversing the car then drawing out of the gates onto the road, 'chronic emphysema and a terminal cancer case—last stages. Oh, and I want to pop into the hospital on the way back to see another patient who's just had a hysterectomy.'

'Usual mixed bag, then,' he said.

She nodded, and asked curiously, 'If you were at your station what would be a typical morning for you?'

'Well, we don't do too many house calls.' He grinned. 'If we did, all our time would be spent travelling. Some villages can be fifty miles away or even more. We had a woman once who carried her child nearly seventy miles so that he could be treated by us.'

'Did you save him?'

He shook his head. 'Unfortunately, no. He was dead by the time she got there, but I'm afraid that happens quite often. But getting back to your question of a typical morning, how about a new baby, a case of lung disease, an old man dying. . .'

Kate smiled. 'Point taken. I guess it's like you said before. People's needs and problems are the same wherever they are.'

Today the friction which had been between them when he had sat in on her surgery seemed to have gone. He didn't interfere, not with her diagnoses or even to push his own point of view. In fact, quite the reverse was the case, and as she watched him as he held the newborn baby, gave a few words of encouragment to the emphysema case and extended compassion to the terminal patient she was struck by his gentleness and apparent humility.

The fears she'd had about him the previous night seemed so improbable now that she felt half-ashamed she'd even harboured such thoughts. By the time they reached the hospital she was beginning to think that she even quite liked him, in spite of his scruffy appearance and laid-back manner.

The woman who'd had the hysterectomy the previous day was still quite poorly but she was pleased to see Kate.

'Hello, Dr Chapman.' She struggled to sit up but Kate held up her hand to deter her. 'How nice of you to come.'

'How are you, Marjorie?' asked Kate.

'Pretty groggy, really. I still feel queasy from the anaesthetic and the wound is painful, especially around the drain they've put in.'

'You're bound to feel like that for a day or two,' said Kate. 'On the way in I saw the registrar who performed your operation. He said you had several very large fibroids, as we had suspected. Just think, Marjorie, that's an end now to all that heavy bleeding.'

'I know. I can hardly believe it.' In spite of her discomfort, the woman looked pleased. Her gaze flickered to Jon Hammond.

'I'm sorry, Marjorie,' said Kate, who was beginning by now to recognise that interested look. 'This is Dr Hammond. He is with us for a while as Dr Wooldridge's locum.'

Jon spoke to the patient while Kate studied her observations chart and when they left the ward a few minutes later Kate had the distinct impression that Marjorie was feeling far more cheerful than when they had arrived, but she also had the sneaking feeling that that fact was due more to Jon Hammond's presence than to anything she herself might have said.

CHAPTER FOUR

IT WAS almost lunchtime and for the first time that day the crowd in the accident and emergency waiting room began to clear. Helen Turner glanced at the fob watch on the front of her uniform and was just wondering if she dared go to the hospital canteen and grab herself a sandwich before the next onslaught when through the revolving glass doors in the main foyer she caught sight of Kate Chapman and Jon Hammond, who also seemed to be heading in the direction of the canteen.

After a quick word with Stephanie Miles, the other sister on her unit, Helen hurried through the corridors to the canteen. She saw Kate and Jon immediately. They had bought lunch and were sitting at a table in the window. They saw her and Kate waved, beckoning for her to join them. She waved back, bought herself a salad sandwich, some fruit and a cup of tea at the counter, then carried her tray to the window seat.

'To what do we owe this honour?' she said. 'A visit from not one, but two GPs.'

Kate laughed and as Helen sat down she said, 'I had to visit a patient on Gynae so as we'd almost finished house calls we thought we might as well take advantage of your facilities.'

'And why not?' Helen smiled, noticing that Jon Hammond looked different from the night before when she had shown him round the stable flat, although for the moment she couldn't quite put her finger on what it was.

52

She had liked the new locum on sight, liked his easygoing manner and friendly approach, and she had no qualms about him staying in the flat. 'So, how was the Thistle and Rose?' she asked.

Jon grinned. 'Well, their food was excellent but it seems I wasn't destined to try out their accommodation.'

'Really? Why not?' Helen glanced from Jon to Kate, then back to Jon again.

'They were full.' He shrugged. 'Cyclists, I understand, taking part in some race.'

'Oh, yes. I'd forgotten about that,' said Helen. 'So what happened—where are you staying?'

'Very comfortable digs,' said Jon solemnly. 'Luxury apartment. All mod cons, even a sea view.'

'Heavens,' said Helen. 'That must be costing you a fortune. Where is it exactly?'

'Right on the seafront at Cowes,' Jon replied.

'On the seafront? You mean. . .?' Helen trailed off as she realised what he meant, and threw Kate a quick look. She was amused to see that Kate's cheeks had grown quite pink.

'We didn't have a lot of choice,' Kate replied primly. 'It was very late and the cyclists seem to have taken over the entire Island.'

'I offered to sleep on the beach,' said Jon, 'but Kate wouldn't hear of it.'

'I should think not,' said Helen. 'So what will you do tonight and possibly tomorrow? I don't think the painters will be finished before then.'

'I think that's rather up to Kate,' Jon replied.

'Well, you can stay,' she replied, a little huffily Helen thought. 'I thought I'd already made that plain.'

He grinned and winked at her, and the colour on her cheeks deepened even more.

Helen watched in delighted amazement. It had been a very long time since she'd seen her friend affected in that way by a man. Alistair Cunningham had been the last, but that had been a long time ago and had ended very abruptly. Kate had never told her why, but Helen suspected her friend had been badly hurt. It would be nice to see some romance in her life again.

She looked back at Jon and realised quite suddenly what was different about him. He'd had his hair cut. Bleached by the sun, it was still on the longish side, but newly washed it shone and looked less straggly and unkempt than before.

'Isn't that Andrew Merrick over there?' Kate's question suddenly broke into Helen's thoughts. Glancing over her shoulder to see where Kate was looking, Helen had the distinct impression she'd deliberately changed the subject.

'Yes, that's him,' she agreed. For Jon's benefit she added, 'He's our casualty officer.'

'So, what about these rumours I've been hearing?' asked Kate.

'If you mean about him and Georgina,' said Helen quickly, 'then they aren't rumours. They happen to be true.'

'Sounds intriguing,' observed Jon, leaning back in his chair.

'It is,' said Helen, 'although not in the way you may think. Andrew and Georgina Merrick were married. They got divorced about a couple of years ago but just recently Georgina, who is a staff nurse, came back to work on A and E and she and Andrew have got back together again. They are remarrying at Easter.'

'I think that's really neat,' said Jon slowly.

'Well, it certainly make a change these days to hear something like that,' agreed Kate. 'I'm so pleased for them and for their girls. They have two daughters,' she added to Jon. 'Lauren and Natasha. They are lovely children.' As she finished speaking she glanced at her watch. 'Well,' she said, rising to her feet, 'this is all very pleasant, I'm sure, but we really must be getting on. We have one more house call and then I have a clinic to take.'

Jon looked a bit startled by the suddenness of Kate's actions, but he drained his cup and he, too, rose. 'Nice talking to you again, Helen,' he said. 'I'll see you in a day or so.'

'Yes, fine,' Helen replied. 'I'll give you a ring either at the surgery or, I presume, at Kate's.'

He grinned again and nodded. He really was quite attractive in a very weathered, rugged sort of way, Helen decided as thoughtfully she watched the pair of them leave the canteen. Not, she would have said, Kate's usual type at all, but you never could tell. It was so often true about opposites being attracted to each other.

Secretly Helen knew she would love to see Kate settle down with the right man. She had changed in recent years from the fun-loving girl she had been in their schooldays. Not that people stayed the same for ever. No doubt in Kate's eyes she, too, had changed, Helen thought with a sign, but there was a seriousness about Kate these days that she had wondered about. Once she had tried to broach the matter during lunch and a gossip, but Kate had dismissed her querying with an uncharacteristic brusqueness which had only served to make Helen wonder all the more.

Current developments, however, certainly looked as if they could be interesting, if not downright promising.

Helen finished her lunch, then stood up and prepared once more to enter the fray of Casualty.

'Where are we going?' asked Jon as they drew out of the hospital car park.

'I want to visit a patient in Porchfield,' Kate replied. 'She's elderly and housebound, and I visit once a month.'

She didn't tell him that she hadn't intended visiting that day, that she had only said it to escape from Helen's speculative look. Helen knew her too well and had shown far too much interest in the fact that Jon was staying at her apartment. Not that there was any justification for her speculation, of course, but there had been something in the way that Helen had looked at her, then at Jon Hammond and back at her again which had made Kate feel decidedly uncomfortable. It was almost as if Helen was looking at a situation and reading something into it that certainly wasn't there.

Helen meant well but she was a bit of a matchmaker, and Kate knew she would like nothing better than to try to arrange a romance for her. But if she was intending that between herself and Jon Hammond she could certainly think again. They had nothing in common—were like chalk and cheese, really—and it wasn't even as if she found him attractive. Why, he wasn't even her type—not that she was entirely sure quite what her type was these days.

Alistair, she'd thought, had been her type.

She hadn't told Helen what had happened. Helen had wondered. Kate knew that, but she hadn't been able to bring herself to even tell her. . .her best friend. . .

'Why is she housebound?' Jon suddenly broke into her thoughts.

'What?' she said, startled, his intrusion almost a physical thing.

'Your patient,' said Jon. 'Why is she housebound?'

With a start Kate realised she had become so lost in her thoughts that she'd driven from Shalbrooke into the village of Porchfield without even being aware of it.

'She has pernicious anaemia,' she said. 'I call in once a month to give her a vitamin B12 injection.'

The house was large, set back from the road behind a red brick wall and situated at the end of a drive lined with neatly clipped privet hedges. Immaculate lawns surrounded large flower-beds packed with polyanthus, daffodils and narcissi.

'Your housebound lady likes gardening,' observed Jon as Kate, with a crunching of gravel, brought the car to a halt before the front door.

'Oh, she doesn't do it,' said Kate quickly. 'She couldn't. She has a gardener.'

'Really?' Jon raised his eyebrows and there was something in his manner that for one moment caused Kate to wonder whether or not she should let him come inside with her.

They got out of the car and before Kate had time to say anything the door opened and two Pekingese rushed out, yapping madly and circling around her, Jon and the car.

'Chang! Ming! Quiet, please! Do you hear me?'

Kate looked up and saw that her patient, Mrs Digby-Smythe, had appeared in the open doorway. Tall and very thin, her white hair beautifully styled, she leaned heavily on a silver-topped walking stick as she called the dogs, at the same time peering imperiously at Kate and at Jon Hammond.

'Oh, Katherine,' she said at last, 'it's you. I wasn't expecting you today.'

'Hello, Mrs Digby-Smythe,' said Kate cheerfully. 'I was in the area and thought I would—'

'You'd better come in.' Not giving Kate the chance to say more, or even to introduce Jon, the old lady turned and went back down the hall followed by the dogs, still yapping wildly.

'I think I'll stay here,' said Jon, settling himself against the bonnet of the car.

'OK.' Kate smiled and followed her patient into the house, down the thickly carpeted hallway and into a drawing room packed with antique furniture and Chinese artefacts.

'Was that young man your driver?' The inevitable question came as Kate was drawing up the vitamin injection. 'I sympathise with you.' The old lady swept on, not giving Kate a chance to answer as she rolled up the sleeve of her violet cashmere cardigan. 'It's impossible to get staff these days, you know, and then one can't be sure who one's getting. Scruffy individuals for the most part. No pride. No respect. Where did you find him, my dear? You really can't be too careful, you know. One hears such stories.'

'But he isn't my driver,' said Kate, as she swabbed her patient's arm with cotton wool soaked in antiseptic solution.

'He isn't?' The old lady looked more imperious than ever as she peered down her aquiline nose.

Kate shook her head. 'I don't have a driver. I prefer to drive myself.'

'So who is he?'

'He's a doctor.'

'A doctor!'

The dogs yelped and Kate felt her lips twitch at the startled horror in the old lady's tone.

'Dressed like that?'

'You should have seen him when he first arrived.' Kate chuckled.

'Has he joined the practice?' demanded Mrs Digby-Smythe.

'Temporarily,' Kate replied. 'He's a locum for Dr Wooldridge. Now, hold still, please. Just a little scratch. . . there. . .that's it.' She withdrew the needle. 'That's over for another month. Tell me, how have you been feeling?'

But Mrs Digby-Smythe hadn't finished. 'What does Richard say about this?' she demanded.

'Nothing, really.' Kate shrugged. 'I think he's just pleased to have some help.'

'It wouldn't have happened in his father's day.' The old lady snorted in disgust. 'Doctors were dignified in those days—respected. They came from families with breeding. . .good backgrounds. . . Nowadays. . .well! Anything goes!'

'I don't think you'll find there's too much wrong with Dr Hammond.' To her amazement, Kate heard herself defending him. 'And his appearance is probably down to the fact that he's just returned from Africa.'

'That may be so.' Mrs Digby-Smythe stood up. 'But that doesn't give him the right to wear those dreadful denim jeans when he's doing house calls.'

'Everyone wears them these days,' said Kate with a smile.

'Precisely,' snapped the old lady. 'That's exactly my meaning. It's just another example of standards having dropped, and when standards drop ruin follows.'

'Maybe, maybe not,' said Kate. 'But you still haven't answered my question. I want to know how you've been feeling.'

'Tired. Always tired. But, apart from this wretched anaemia, I'm as fit as a fiddle.'

'Good,' said Kate. 'I'm glad to hear it. Now, I'll see myself out. You keep the dogs in here, otherwise they'll chase the car down the drive.'

'Very well. Goodbye, Katherine. You'll call again next month?'

'Of course,' Kate replied. 'Unless you need me before.'

Outside she found Jon, still leaning against the car. His arm were folded, his long legs thrust out and his trainers were digging deep grooves in the gravel. 'All done?' he said as she closed the front door behind her.

She nodded and opened the car door. He pushed himself upright and turned to gaze up at the house. 'Weathly folk?' he said as he slipped into the passenger seat beside her.

'Very,' Kate replied. 'Her husband was a high court judge but her own family were wealthy land-owners, something to do with tea plantations, I believe.'

He grimaced as she started the car and drew away. 'I thought as much,' he said. 'I recognised the look she gave me. I've seen it many times in Africa.'

Kate didn't answer. They remained in silence for a few minutes but after they had driven out onto the main road and left the house behind them Jon spoke again. 'Why doesn't she come to the centre for her injections?'

'I told you, she's practically housebound these days.'

'Doesn't she have a car?'

'Not now. No.'

'Couldn't she get a taxi? After all, it isn't as if she couldn't afford it.'

'I don't know, Jon.' Suddenly Kate began to feel irritated. She'd defended him to Mrs Digby-Smythe and now here she was, defending her patient to him. 'She's always had a house call. For as long as I can remember.'

'Would you extend that courtesy to all your patients in a similar situation?'

'Of course. I would like to think I—'

'She's not an NHS patient, of course.'

Kate took a deep breath. She'd been waiting for that. 'No,' she said, 'she's a private patient.'

'Ah.' That was all he said. That was all he had to say for there was a wealth of innuendo in that one word.

There was a further silence as they drove back to the centre. As they passed the hospital Jon said, 'I find this life of privilege a bit difficult to handle after where I've been.'

'I hope you don't think Mrs Digby-Smythe is typical of our average patient,' Kate retorted, 'because she isn't. Not by any means. But she is a patient, whatever her circumstances. She is very frail and she deserves the same respect as anyone else.'

'I wasn't only referring to her situation,' he said.

'What do you mean?' She threw him a quick glance as she drove into the Fleetwood's car park and switched off the engine.

'I was talking about everything that makes up the picture here,' he replied. 'Large modern hospital, fund-holding group practice. Luxury apartments. Company-owned yachts. Membership of the golf club. . . Private schools. . . All that adds up to privilege beyond the wildest dreams of the people I treat.'

Kate turned to look at him and saw that he was staring out of the windscreen with that far-away expression in his eyes once again, as if he was focussing on some distant horizon.

'Most of my patients,' he went on after a moment, 'have to walk up to twenty miles just to draw their daily water—and that's the women. They sleep on cane matting on the ground. They give birth to their babies in a ditch behind the nearest convenient bush. They bury as many children as survive. Most of their lives are spent in poverty, fighting pain and disease. . .' He broke off, his voice catching in his throat. 'But I guess that's the way of the world,' he added a moment later. 'We can't change it single-handed, much as we'd sometimes like to. . . Right, so what next?'

He turned and looked at her but for the moment Kate was lost for words, silenced by his sudden, passionate outburst—over as suddenly as it had begun. She'd had no idea he felt so deeply and so strongly. But how could she? She knew so little about him, about what made him tick—even about what made him live the life he chose.

'I have my Well Woman clinic,' she said slowly.

'Oh, yes. I'd forgotten. Well, maybe I could sit in. If you have no objections, that is. We have been talking of setting up something similar at the station and it would be nice to see how you do it.' She hadn't the heart to refuse and he followed her through Reception to her consulting room.

'So, tell me, what does this clinic consist of?' he asked.

'Cervical smears,' said Kate, and breast checks for any lumps or abnormalities, which would then be referred to the mammography unit. Contraceptive advice and monitoring, blood-pressure checks. Pregnancy advice—sometimes leading to a termination at one end of the scale or IVF treatment, where appropriate, at the other. But I think the thing to do,' she added, 'is to get started, then you can see for yourself.'

The first patient was a young woman who was living with her boyfriend and who had two children from a previous relationship. She was seeking contraceptive advice.

'My boyfriend is keen to have a child,' she said, 'but I don't want any more. I'm hoping I'll be able to talk him into having a vasectomy eventually, but he isn't keen so for the time being I think I'd better go on the Pill.'

After Kate had carried out the usual blood-pressure check, weighed the patient and asked all the routine questions concerning health and hereditary factors, she prescribed a low-dosage brand of the contraceptive pill.

'Thanks, Dr Chapman,' the young woman said. Just before she left the room she added, 'I'll try and talk Lee into coming in to see you.'

As the door closed behind the woman Kate looked up and saw some emotion pass across Jon's face, an emotion which could almost have been a shudder.

'What's wrong?' she demanded.

He shook his head. 'I was just thinking of that poor guy,' he said. 'Not only does he not have children of his own but she is about to make sure once and for all that he never does.'

'At least she's showing a sense of responsibility,' retorted Kate. 'A lot we see don't even think about it until it's too late.'

Jon shrugged. 'It might have made a bit more sense if he'd been her husband but, you have to admit, it's a pretty drastic measure for just another casual relationship.'

The second patient was a young girl, accompanied by her mother, who was requesting that her daughter be put on the Pill. 'Just to be on the safe side, Doctor,' she said seriously. 'She's started going out with boys, and you can't be too careful, can you?'

'Well,' said Jon cynically, as the pair left the room with a prescription, 'if that isn't a licence to kill I don't know what is.'

'What do you mean?' demanded Kate angrily.

'If that young lady hasn't had sex before she certainly will now.'

'Look,' said Kate angrily, 'if all you are going to do is to sit there and criticise, then I would rather you left the room and let me get on with this clinic on my own. My job is hard enough as it is, without you sticking your oar in.'

'Sorry.' He held up his hands in defence. 'I won't say another word, I promise.'

Kate didn't answer, but began to shuffle through the next patient's records.

'Can I stay? Please?' he asked.

'What?' She looked up angrily.

'If I behave? Can I stay?'

'Oh, I suppose so! But you sit there quietly and don't interfere or criticise. Is that clear?'

He nodded and she pressed the buzzer.

Somehow she got through the rest of the clinic. She performed several cervical smears and continued to issue family-planning advice. True to his word, Jon didn't interfere or even comment any further, and when at last Claire rang through to say there were no more patients Kate leaned back in her chair with a sigh.

'Well, that's that,' she said. Throwing him a curious glance, she said, 'So, have you learnt anything? Do you think you could use any of that in your bush station?'

'Difficult to say.'

'Do you give contraceptive advice?'

'Yes. . . But—'

'I should have thought it's essential in countries suffering from over-population and famines.'

'Maybe.' He shrugged. 'But in my experience neither the amount of advice you offer nor the number of contraceptives you hand out make the slightest bit of difference if the people concerned refuse to use them.'

'But why wouldn't they use them?' Kate stared at him. 'I would have thought they would be only too pleased to limit the number of children they have.'

'It's not that straightforward.' He shook his head. 'It's in their culture to have large families.'

'You mean on religious grounds?'

'Not necessarily. Take the villages around the bush station where I'm working at the moment, for example. A man from one of those villages demonstrates his prowess by the number of children he produces.'

'And what about the women?' demanded Kate. 'Would they agree with that concept, I wonder.'

'You'd be surprised. Their babies are their lives. The size of their families is almost a status symbol. You also have to remember that a lot of babies die at birth, or in infancy, so the more they produce the better the chance of several surviving into adulthood. Believe me, Kate, it's their way. I've seen the misery if babies don't come along. And there's no expensive IVF treatment in the middle of the bush.'

'How do they cope?' Suddenly Kate was curious about this different, almost alien way of life. 'If a woman can't have children, I mean?'

'They share,' said Jon. 'The childless woman will take

on responsibility for helping to care for her sister's children or the children from her husband's family. In that way some of her longings are assuaged.'

'I see.' Kate fell silent. 'You make it all sound ideal. But I doubt it is in reality.'

'I sometimes doubt the problems are any worse than those created by so-called civilised society,' said Jon. 'They have, for example, a very strong moral code. Illigitimacy is frowned upon and sex outside marriage is punishable.'

'Heavens!' said Kate. 'Imagine trying to impose those sorts of restrictions here.'

'Yes,' said Jon. 'Just imagine.' He grinned. 'That's not to say that those sorts of things don't go on because, of course, they do. But maybe not on quite such a grand scale.' He yawned suddenly and stretched. 'Is that it, then, for today?'

'Yes.' Kate nodded.

'Good. That means we can go home.'

She stiffened slightly at the familiarity in his tone. 'Yes,' she agreed at last, 'I suppose it does.'

'Can I cook supper?'

'Yes, of course you can,' she replied, wondering if he thought her so unreasonable that she would not let him use her kitchen. At that moment the intercom sounded on her desk. 'What is it, Claire?' she asked.

'Call from the community nurse, Dr Chapman. Tom Ashton is deteriorating rapidly.'

'Right, Claire, thank you,' said Kate. 'Tell them I'm on my way.'

'Tom Ashton?' said Jon quickly, 'the terminal cancer case we visited?'

Kate nodded. 'Final stages, by the sounds of it.'

'You want me to come with you?'

She shook her head. 'No, the family will be having enough to cope with, without two of us turning up. I'll drop you off at the apartment first. Here's my key,' she added, detaching it from her keyring and handing it across the desk.

He hesitated, and for one moment Kate thought he was going to refuse and insist on accompanying her. She was tired and hadn't the energy for a battle so she was relieved when at last he nodded and took the key.

CHAPTER FIVE

TOM Ashton's family was grouped around his bed—his wife, Jill, their two sons and their daughter. Tom's brother, Brian, was also there, and so were his four grandchildren who, although not actually in the room, were elsewhere in the house.

'I'm sorry, Doctor.' Jill attempted to apologise for the lack of space when she caught sight of Kate, but Kate brushed her apology aside.

'I like to see a family around at a time like this,' she said. 'It shows love and a closeness which can sometimes be missing on these occasions.'

'Tom wanted to be at home,' said Jill simply.

'I know he did,' Kate replied, 'and you've made that possible.'

'He's not suffering, is he?' Jill threw an agonised glance at the man on the bed.

Kate shook her head. 'He's deeply unconscious, Jill.'

Jill Ashton sighed and gripped her elder son's hand. 'He rallied for a little while this afternoon after Steve and his family arrived,' she said quietly.

'So he knows that everyone he loves is around him,' said Kate.

Jill didn't answer but carried on watching her husband, as if trying to imprint these last precious moments on her mind. After a while Kate slipped out of the room, motioning for Alison, the community nurse, to join her.

'He's deteriorated rapidly since about five o'clock,'

said Alison, closing the door behind her. 'I've maintained the diamorphine dose but his lungs are filling.'

'It won't be long,' said Kate. She spoke quietly so that none of the family would overhear. 'I think I'll stay,' she added. 'I'm a bit concerned about Jill.'

'I know,' said Alison. 'She's been an absolute tower of strength throughout all this. Right since Tom was diagnosed she's been there for everyone. I only hope afterwards her children will be there for her.'

'Excuse me, Doctor.' Kate looked up to find that Tom's brother had come out of the bedroom.

'Yes, Brian,' she said. 'What is it?'

'I was wondering whether there was anything else that could be done for Tom?'

'In what way, Brian?' Kate said gently.

'Well, you do hear sometimes. . .these last-minute miracles. . .perhaps another sort of treatment. . . It might not be too late to operate, even. I never did understand why they didn't operate. . .'

Kate, recognising the desperate look in the man's eyes as one she had seen so many times before on the faces of frantic relatives, stood up and put her hand on his arm.

Without a word, Alison went back into the bedroom.

'I'm sorry, Brian,' said Kate, 'but there really isn't anything else to be done.'

Tears welled in the man's eyes and he swallowed deeply. 'I can't believe it,' he choked. 'It seems like only yesterday we were nippers together, scrumping for apples and running away from the village bobby.'

'I know, Brian, I know, and those memories will always be special for you.'

'But he's only fifty-six, damn it! That's no age, Doctor. Not these days it isn't. He's much too young to die. He hadn't even reached retirement yet. Why should his life be cut short now?'

'Life can be cruel,' Kate agreed, 'but it sometimes helps to think of it not as a life cut short but as a life complete—that fifty-six years was the span for Tom.'

Brian looked bewildered but Kate hoped that later he might remember what she'd said. At that moment Alison appeared in the bedroom doorway again, and one look at her expression told Kate the end had come for Tom Ashton.

'Come on, Brian,' she said taking his arm again. 'We are both needed.'

It was quite dark by the time Kate left the Ashtons' house. She took the coast road home past Egypt Point. She felt drained, not only from dealing with Tom Ashton's death but also with coping with his family's loss and devastation.

Jill had refused her offer of sedatives, and secretly Kate had been pleased. Jill had appeared calm and accepting of the situation, and although Kate knew the moment of realisation would come when she would be swamped by her grief she also knew from experience that sedatives would only serve to prolong that moment and not banish it completely.

It was a still, starlit night, the sea calm after the tempestuous waves of the previous night. Now the surf broke on the shingle in little frills of white lace, and the moon formed a silver pathway from the Island to Southampton Water. A brightly lit P&O ferry glided soundlessly through the Solent like some huge, floating towerblock, while around the harbour fishing boats and dinghies tugged gently at their moorings and bobbed up and down in the slight swell.

With a sudden pang, Kate wondered what Jon was doing. It seemed strange to be going home, knowing someone was there. That hadn't happened for a very long time. A slight tremor rippled through her at the memory, and once again she found herself wishing she had insisted that he made other arrangements.

He seemed all right, she had to admit. In fact, there appeared to be more depth to him than she would have believed possible. First appearances could certainly be deceptive. But, on the other hand, when she'd met Alistair she had been completely taken in, even though in that instance it had been by his charm, his wit, his public-school education and his impeccable background. And those opinions she'd formed had been wrong, so totally wrong. Could she maybe have been wrong in thinking that Jon Hammond was little more than a scruffy drifter?

With a sigh, she drove along the seafront and approached her apartment block. Glancing up at the front façade, she saw that the lights were burning and in spite of her misgivings it was somehow welcoming. At the same time, however, she realised she had been hoping he might have eaten by now and gone to his room.

Having parked the car, she rested her arms on the steering-wheel for a moment. Would she never be free of this legacy of fear she'd inherited from Alistair? Would she never be able to trust anyone again?

At last, knowing she could delay the moment no longer, she got out of the car and let herself into the apartment. A delicious savoury smell wafted down the stairs to greet her.

She found Jon in the kitchen. Barefoot and wearing a

white T-shirt tucked into his jeans, he was standing in front of the cooker. A quick intrigued glance revealed to Kate pots and pans on the stove, their contents simmering, while on the worktop red wine breathed gently in an open bottle.

'Good,' he said, barely looking up as expertly he wielded the contents of her frying pan. 'I'm glad you're here. I would have had to have turned this lot off if you'd been any longer. Glass of wine?'

She stood in the doorway and stared around her kitchen. She doubted whether it had seen such activity for a very long time, if at all. 'Haven't you eaten?' she asked faintly.

'Of course not,' he replied, glancing at her for the first time. 'You look shattered,' he added bluntly.

'I am.'

'Tom Ashton?' His raised eyebrows indicated anticipation.

'Yes. About an hour ago. It's been rough on his family.'

'You do need that drink.' Turning to the worktop, he poured red wine into two glasses and handed one to her.

'Thanks.' She nodded, put her case onto the floor and took a sip of the wine. It seemed to flow into her veins. Setting the glass down, she said, 'You've cooked for me?'

'Yes. What did you think I meant when I asked to use the kitchen?'

She shrugged. 'I don't know, really. I suppose I thought you meant you just wanted to cook something for yourself.'

'That wouldn't have been very civil. Especially as you've been working and it's your flat and you've been good enough to let me stay.'

She had a sudden mental picture of Alistair demanding a meal after she'd had a particularly heavy shift at the hospital. Dismissing the image, she said, 'Give me a moment to freshen up.'

In the bedroom she slipped off her suit and pulled on a sapphire-blue sweatshirt and trousers in soft velour. In the bathroom she splashed her face with cold water and combed her hair, then found herself applying just a touch of make-up—lipstick, mascara and finally a quick spray of perfume.

He had set the dining table in the window. The curtains were thrown back, revealing the night view of the Solent, and after he had indicated to Kate to take her place he served the first course—warm pitta bread and a spicy dip.

It wasn't until Kate began to eat that she realised how hungry she was. She'd had nothing since the sandwich in the hospital canteen at lunchtime, and now it was after nine o'clock. They spoke little as they ate the starter, then went on to the main course of a chicken and red pepper stir-fry, together with the remainder of the red wine.

'This is wonderful,' sighed Kate at last. 'I'm not going to ask where you learned to cook, but I am intrigued where you obtained the ingredients.'

He leaned back in his chair, twirling the stem of his wine glass and watching the contents stain the sides of the glass. 'I bought it all this morning,' he said, 'when I went shopping. I must say, the guy in the off-licence knows his stuff—this wine is excellent.'

'Better than the average bush station plonk?' said Kate, with just a hint of mischief in her tone.

'Infinitely!' He laughed.

'That makes a change.'

'What do you mean?' he protested, staring at her across the table.

'Well, you've compared just about everything else that

I've said or done today to the African experience, even down to the advice I've given in surgery. And most, it would appear, you've found wanting so it comes as a pleasant surprise that our wine is superior.'

'You make me sound a right pompous prig.'

'Not really.' She grinned. 'At least, I didn't mean it to come out that way.'

'You should do that more often.'

'What?' She looked up quickly.

'Smile,' he said. 'It lights up your face. And while we're on the subject, you should wear that colour more often as well—it's the exact blue of your eyes.'

'Is that a fact?' She knew an edge of sarcasm had crept into her voice.

'It's an unusual combination with your dark hair,' he went on, apparently unperturbed. 'Do you have Irish blood. . .or Welsh, maybe?' he added when she shrugged and shook her head. 'I knew a Welsh woman once with black hair and those blue eyes. . .' A dreamy look came into his eyes as if he reminisced in some private fantasy. When Kate emphatically shook her head he sighed and said, 'No? Oh, well, never mind. It's devastating, wherever it comes from. But no doubt you've been told that. Many times.'

'Not that many. No.'

'Then I can't imagine what the men of the Wight are thinking about.'

Suddenly Kate felt embarrassed, not just by what he was implying but by the expression in his eyes as he coolly surveyed her. It was as if that steady grey stare could see into her heart, into her very soul, stripping it bare and exposing all her fears. It was disconcerting, to say the least, and abruptly she stood up and began collecting the plates.

'Why the sudden hurry?' he said, looking up at her and narrowing his eyes.

'It's getting late.'

'Not that late.'

'Late enough. I'll make the coffee.' She made her escape to the kitchen and left him still sitting at the table, leaning dangerously back in his chair.

He followed her after a few minutes, as she'd known he would—just as he had done the night before—but this time she was ready for him and didn't jump violently when he suddenly appeared in the open doorway.

'Why do you lock your bedroom door?' he asked, the unexpectedness of the question taking her breath away so that for almost a full minute she stopped what she was doing and stared at the kettle and mugs in front of her.

Slowly she turned and looked at him. He was leaning against the doorframe, watching her, one arm above his head. The pose could have been nonchalant but the expression in his eyes was too perceptive.

'How did you know?'

'That it was locked? Because I heard you turn the key. I'm intrigued. Do you always lock it, or was it because of me?'

She took a deep breath and the rich aroma of the coffee filled her lungs. 'I heard a story once,' she said, 'about a friend who woke to find an intruder actually in her room. . .'

'And since then you've always locked your bedroom door at night?'

Squarely she met his gaze. Suddenly to lie was quite impossible. 'No,' she admitted.

'There's no need, you know,' he said, and his voice was low, as soft as the tide as it brushed the shingle.

'I know,' she said. And she did know, she realised with a little sense of shock as she turned away and picked up the tray. This man was safe.

'Do you want to talk about it?' he asked, barring the doorway.

She shook her head. 'No,' she replied.

'OK.' He stood aside but as she passed him, her shoulder brushing his chest, he said softly, 'But if you should change your mind I'm a good listener.'

She didn't lock her door that night, and she slept well. She woke early, however, and for a long time she lay thinking. For the most part her thoughts were of the man who had quite literally ambled into her life and unknowingly had changed something. Kate herself wasn't even entirely sure what that something was—she only knew the balance of something had shifted.

Once again he was already up by the time she emerged from her bedroom, but later, after she'd showered and dressed, there was no sign of him and the apartment was silent. He'd obviously made tea because the kettle was still hot, but the kitchen was empty.

Kate had just come to the conclusion that he must have gone out when she wandered into the sitting room and caught sight of him through the picture window.

He was on the beach, right at the water's edge, arms akimbo as he stared across the Solent towards the mainland. She wondered what he was thinking—whether he really was appreciating the view or whether his mind was far away in the vast open spaces of the African bush where, it seemed, his heart was.

He was a strange man in many ways, different from any man she'd known before, and the exact opposite of Alistair. Even physically they were different. Jon was tall and fair, where Alistair had been dark and of a stocky build. His eyes were grey, and Alistair's had been brown. . .

She shivered suddenly. Why was she comparing them? Why was she even thinking of Alistair?

She was about to turn away from the window when Jon suddenly picked up a pebble from the beach and sent it skimming across the water. She watched as it bounced two, three, four times and found herself rooted to the spot, unable to move, as he sent another and then another across the waves, his body bending and flexing and the muscles rippling in his arms and shoulders.

Even when, unexpectedly, he turned his head and caught sight of her standing there in the window, watching him, she felt powerless to move.

He raised his hand, and loped easily back up the beach over the pebbles and the sea wall and then across the road. Only when he had entered the apartment and was out of her sight did she seem able to move, and by then she could already hear him on the stairs.

As he strode into the room she turned to face him, suddenly overcome with embarrassment that he should have caught her watching him. He had been about to speak but something in her expression must have caused the words to die on his lips. Instead, he stopped and raised his eyebrows questioningly.

For a long moment they simply stared at each other, then softly he said, 'Is there anything wrong?'

'No. No.' Quickly Kate turned away and began to straighten the cushions on the sofa, which were in no need whatsoever of being straightened. 'No, there's nothing wrong. I. . .should be making a move if I'm not going to be late for work, that's all.'

'I'm ready when you are,' he said in the same soft tones.

That day followed much the same pattern as the previous one, with Jon familiarising himself with procedures at the centre and accompanying Kate on her house calls.

Although very aware of his presence, the experience seemed for Kate to have lost something of the abrasive quality of the previous day, and by the end she was forced to admit she had enjoyed his company.

That evening she found herself not only honour-bound to cook supper for them both after Jon's efforts of the previous night but actually wanting to. She cooked a rack of lamb with fresh vegetables and opened a bottle of wine, just as he had done.

'That was excellent,' he said afterwards, leaning back in his chair and surveying her through half-closed eyelids.

'You're welcome.' Suddenly she felt ridiculously pleased, but she realised with a slight shock that she meant it.

She was still wary of him but, then, she would have been of any man staying in her home, but by that third night she was certainly far more comfortable than she had been at first.

The following morning being Saturday, had less of a sense of urgency, and it was while they were lingering over toast, coffee and the morning papers that the phone rang.

'Kate, it's Helen. Thought I'd give you a ring to say that the painters have finished and that Jon can move in just as soon as he likes.'

'Oh, right, Helen. I'll tell him.' Her eyes met Jon's across the table. 'He's right here.' As she replaced the receiver she said, 'The flat's ready. Helen says you can move in.'

'I see.' Some emotion crossed his features, an expression which Kate found impossible to define. 'Well, I won't need to impose on you any more.'

'Would you like me to run you over to Gatcombe?' she said.

'Thanks, but I'm sure you have better things to do with your weekend. I could get a cab.'

She shook her head. 'It's no problem,' she said. 'I have to go shopping anyway. I can drop you off and go on to the supermarket.'

'OK, then.' He seemed pleased, but Kate couldn't be sure. 'If you're certain. I'll get my gear.'

She cleared the table and went to the bedroom to fetch her jacket, bag and car keys. When she returned she found him standing at the window with his bags on the floor beside him, together with the boots and the dark green bush hat.

Pausing in the doorway, she watched him and suddenly an unfamiliar sensation flooded over her. She couldn't identify it—it seemed to be a combination of tenderness and compassion—and just for the moment it was as if she didn't want him to go. Had it only been three days ago that he'd moved in? It seemed he had been here for ever.

'It's fascinating, isn't it—the sea?' he said, without turning, as he sensed her presence.

'I never tire of watching it,' she replied, trying to overcome the emotions she had felt. 'It has so many moods.'

'A bit like a woman.' He did turn then, his eyes meeting

hers. 'Wild and tempestuous at times, at others soft and gentle.'

She could have been forgiven for thinking he mocked her. After all, it wouldn't have been the first time. But there was no trace of mockery now, either in his clear grey eyes or in his tone. Even as she searched for something to say he took her hand and held it.

'Thank you, Kate,' he said simply, 'for letting me stay. I really do appreciate it, you know.' Bending over her hand, he raised it to his lips.

'That's all right. . .' Her voice was suddenly husky and she found herself gazing at the honey-coloured tangle of his hair as, to her amazement, she realised she meant it.

Then the moment was over as she briskly withdrew her hand and he lifted his head then straightened, before picking up his belongings and following her out of the apartment.

There was an early morning mist, but as they headed inland it lifted and all that remained were wraith-like strands that hung low in the valley along the Medina River.

They avoided the bustling market town of Newport and branched off. They skirted Carisbrooke Castle, its battlements sparkling in the March sunshine, before dropping down into the country lanes around Gatcombe.

In the hedgerows bright green buds were poised, set to burst, while along the banks primroses and celandines clustered in thick clumps, and in the fields beyond sheep and cattle grazed quietly.

'I'd forgotten just how beautiful an English spring day can be,' said, Jon gazing out of the car window.

'Maybe that's because you'd wanted to forget.' She had no idea why she'd said it. It just came out. She threw him a sideways glance, expecting him to deny it. But he didn't, remaining silent until, with a small sound that could have been a sigh, he quietly said, 'Maybe I did at that.'

Helen was waiting for them at the the Coach House, but there was no sign of Harry.

'He's still in bed,' Helen replied in answer to Kate's question. 'We've had a dreadful night. He couldn't remember who I was.'

'Do you want me to take a look at him?' asked Kate, getting out of the car and unlocking the boot for Jon to retrieve his bags. She bent down to pat Chester, who had wandered over to investigate the early morning visitors.

'I think I'd rather let him sleep, if you don't mind,' said Helen. She looked pale and drawn and had dark smudges beneath her eyes. 'It's just like having a small child around. I have to watch him almost continuously.' She glanced down at Jon's luggage. 'Is that all you have?' she asked in amazement.

'I travel light,' he grinned.

'Well,' said Kate, 'I suppose I'd better get along.' She didn't want to go. She wanted to stay, for some inexplicable reason, but she couldn't think of any excuse for doing so.

'Oh, don't go yet,' said Helen suddenly, to her relief. 'I'll just show Jon up to the flat then we'll have a coffee.'

'I should be getting on, really,' Kate began, then added helplessly, 'but I dare say I can spare a few minutes.'

She sat down on a wooden bench outside the door and watched as Helen led the way, not into the main building of the house but across the yard to the old ivy-covered coach-house and stables and the flat above. As they climbed the staircase and disappeared inside Kate suddenly felt a totally unreasonable pang of some emotion that felt dangerously akin to jealousy. It was almost as if she resented the enforced intimacy that would inevitably come between Jon Hammond and her friend, living in such close proximity to each other for the next few months.

Which was crazy, really, she told herself firmly, especially as she had been so reluctant to have him stay with her and had been so keen to get rid of him.

'It's good of you to let him have the flat,' she said a little later as she sat in Helen's kitchen and watched her make coffee while Jon unpacked his few belongings.

'Not at all,' Helen replied. 'He's nice. I like him.'

Kate scowled. Inexplicably, she found the idea of Helen liking Jon Hammond quite unattractive. For the past few days he had been her responsibility, even if it had been an unwelcome responsibility.

'And, like I said before,' Helen rattled on completely oblivious to Kate's irrational thoughts, 'it'll be good to have someone else around at this time, with Dad being the way he is. Especially someone who understands.'

'Yes,' agreed Kate, 'yes, of course.' Suddenly she felt ashamed at the thoughts she'd had. Helen was, after all, only trying to help. She didn't have to let Jon use her flat, which she'd already decided to leave empty until her cousin's daughter came to stay. Kate knew she should be grateful to Helen for getting her out of a spot. It could have been difficult finding the locum accommodation at such short notice, especially at the start of the season.

So why was she feeling this way? Almost as if she

resented Helen's involvement—as if she really was jealous, she thought with a jolt.

But why would she be jealous? Helen had Richard. She would hardly be interested in Jon Hammond. And even if she didn't have Richard, and she was interested in Jon Hammond, what possible difference could it make to her, Kate?

She had finished her coffee and was walking back to the car when he came out of the coach house and ambled across the yard to say goodbye.

For a moment he seemed a bit awkward, as if he didn't know quite what to say, then he smiled, that strange, almost lopsided smile of his.

'See you,' he said.

'Yes,' said Kate, equally awkward. 'See you.'

Aware that Helen was standing in the doorway, looking on, Kate quickly got into her car, fastened her seat belt, raised one hand in farewell then drove smartly away.

Driving into town, she had to fight an overwhelming feeling of loneliness. She did her supermarket shopping in a kind of daze, not really caring what she was buying but simply chucking anything into the trolley before driving disconsolately back to Cowes.

The apartment was silent and unbearably empty. Trailing from room to room, she could feel his presence everywhere.

In the kitchen his tall form was leaning over the stove. In the sitting room he sprawled on her sofa or sat at the table in the window, his chair tilted precariously on its back legs.

Disconsolately she stared out at the Solent, busy now with weekend ferries and the first of the season's yachts, but she found no comfort in the usually stimulating scene.

Increasingly restless, she found herself wandering into the bedroom he had used.

He had stripped the divan, and the sheets were neatly folded on top of the duvet. She picked them up and buried her face in them. His scent was there, lingering in the material. The room, though empty, was full of him and the shadow when the curtains fluttered in a sudden breeze could almost have been his.

Many times that day she thought she heard his voice but when she lifted her head to listen, willing him to walk into the room, she knew what she had heard was only the sound of the surf as it broke on the shingle outside the window.

Kate could remember feeling like this only once before in her entire life, and that had been when she had first met Alistair. But she had gone on to fall in love with Alistair, she was telling herself angrily by the end of that miserable Saturday, and there was absolutely no way that this could be happening with Jon Hammond.

She hardly knew the man, for heaven's sake. She had taken an almost instant dislike to him. He wasn't her type and, besides, she had no intention of falling in love with anyone ever again. Not after the last time.

Really, she told herself firmly, she had to pull herself together. She was behaving like a schoolgirl. She had to work alongside this man for some considerable time and, surely, if he had so much as an inkling of the way she was feeling he would no doubt be highly amused. She shuddered at the very thought.

No, she told herself just before she fell asleep that night, the best thing she could do was to act very coolly towards the new locum. Be civil when they met, extend the same courtesy that she would towards any colleague, but at the same time keep out of his way as much as possible.

She slept well and awoke with her new, positive frame of mind still very much intact, but after she'd showered and dressed the day seemed to stretch endlessly before her.

She finished breakfast feeling increasingly restless, wondering how to fill the hours ahead, something that she couldn't ever remember being a problem before. While she was still deliberating the phone rang and she almost jumped out of her skin.

Some sixth sense told her it was Jon. He was phoning to ask what she intended doing with herself that day. Her first instinct was to grab the receiver but she just managed to stop herself. To hold back. She wouldn't want him to think she had been sitting there, expecting him to phone — waiting for him.

On the sixth ring, her heart thumping, she lifted the receiver.

'Hello?' she said, sounding, she hoped, casual.

'Oh, hello. Kate? It's Elizabeth.'

Her heart sank with disappointment.

'Hello, Elizabeth. What can I do for you?'

'I was just phoning to say that Geoff finished fixing my car so the practice car is now free. I wondered if you'd like me to bring it over for Dr Hammond to use.'

'Dr Hammond isn't here now, Elizabeth,' Kate replied. 'He went to Helen Turner's yesterday.'

'Oh, I see. Well, would you like me to take it over to Gatcombe?'

'No, that won't be necessary, Elizabeth,' Kate replied quickly, then heard herself say, 'Maybe if you could bring it here I'll take it over to Gatcombe later today.'

'OK, that's no problem.' Elizabeth sounded relieved, as if she hadn't really wanted to go all the way to Gatcombe. 'But how will you get back?'

'Oh, don't worry about that,' Kate replied airily. 'I'm sure Dr Hammond won't mind running me home.' By the time she replaced the receiver her spirits had soared.

CHAPTER SIX

'DID you sleep well?' Helen, who was weeding the flower-bed by the back door, looked up and sat back on her heels as Jon Hammond strolled across the yard towards her.

'Like a log, thanks.'

'Good.' She smiled. 'First night in a strange bed can sometimes be pretty awful.'

'Not usually for me.' He grinned. 'I can sleep anywhere. This is pure luxury after what I'm used to.'

'I can imagine.' Helen pulled a face. 'Have you got everything you need?'

'Oh, yes, I think so. I live a very simple existence. Like I say, all this luxury—your stable flat and Kate's waterfront apartment—has come as a bit of a culture shock.' He sat down as he spoke on the rustic wooden bench outside the back door and proceeded to watch Helen as she continued with her weeding. 'You Islanders are very privileged people.'

Helen nodded. 'I know.'

'One of the receptionists was telling me there are many Islanders who live out their entire lives here.' He sounded mystified, as if such a concept was entirely beyond his understanding.

'That's true,' Helen agreed, 'and those who do move elsewhere very often only do so for a short time before they return. Many others, of course, have simply chosen to come here to live. Like Kate,' she added.

'Kate?' He frowned. 'Isn't she an Islander?'

'Not strictly speaking,' Helen replied, digging ferociously at a dandelion root.

'But I thought you were at school together.'

'Oh, we were,' she said quickly, 'but Kate was a boarder. Her home was in Dorset. Her parents still live there, but she loved the Island so much she came back and went into partnership with Richard and the others.'

'So, did she know Richard Fleetwood before?'

'Oh, yes.' With a grunt, Helen dislodged the stubborn root and pulled it from the damp earth, sitting back on her heels and surveying it with satisfaction. 'You see, there were three of us at school who were firm friends— Kate, myself and Diana.'

Jon threw her a quick look.

'Diana Parker,' she went on, 'who later became Diana Fleetwood when she married Richard. We were friends at school and stayed friends afterwards. Richard comes from an old Isle of Wight family, and it seemed the most logical thing in the world for him to offer Kate a junior partnership.

'She told me she'd been working in London.'

Glancing up, Helen noticed that Jon had leaned forward with his hands linked loosely between his knees. 'That's right,' she replied. 'She had been working there as an SHO at Barts.'

'Why did she leave?' His voice was soft and Helen, throwing him another glance, could not help but notice the curiosity in the grey eyes.

'I'm not sure, really.' She shrugged. 'I guess it was a combination of several things. I think she'd always hankered to return to the Island. Maybe she'd always secretly wanted to be a GP, although, I have to say, I'd always had the impression she wanted to specialise. . .' She trailed off, suddenly afraid she might be divulging more than she should about her friend.

'But you think there was more to it?'

'Let's say. . .' She hesitated. 'Let just say I think there might have been.'

'You think there might have been a man behind it?'

'I didn't say that,' Helen replied quickly.

'But you suspect it?' he persisted.

She shrugged. 'There was someone,' she agreed, 'and I believe it did all end rather abruptly. But that's all I know.' Scrambling to her feet, she took off her gardening gloves and wiped her palms down the sides of the brown cords she was wearing.

Jon remained silent for a moment, then unexpectedly he said, 'Do you think it could be anything to do with why she is so nervous?'

Helen stared at him in astonishment. 'Nervous?' she said at last. 'Kate?'

'Yes.' He nodded, that straight, slightly unnerving grey gaze meeting hers.

'Kate isn't nervous,' she protested. 'In fact, that's the last way I'd describe her.'

'Are you sure about that?' he said, raising his eyebrows.

'Absolutely,' Helen replied firmly. 'I've known Kate almost for ever. We are friends. I would never, by any stretch of the imagination, describe her as nervous. At school although she was the one with the brains she was also the one with bags of confidence, the one who was always in trouble, if it comes to that—'

'But that was then,' Jon interrupted. 'You are talking about schooldays. That was some little while ago.'

'That's true,' agreed Helen, pulling a face. 'Longer probably than we'd care to admit, but I can't see that—'

'People change.'

'Yes, I know.'

'Things happen to people and they change.'

'But if Kate had changed that much,' Helen protested, 'I would have noticed. We are still friends, after all. We go out together sometimes. . .attend the same parties and functions.'

'And you can honestly say you haven't noticed any change in her?'

'I don't know that I would go that far,' said Helen slowly. 'I guess Kate has matured. We all have. Hopefully. But you are talking nervous here, aren't you?'

He nodded.

'Well, I can't honestly say I've noticed that. She may be quieter, more serious even, but—'

'Maybe she's only nervous at certain times.'

'What do you mean?' Helen stared at him.

'Like when there's a man around?'

'No way!' Helen laughed. 'Kate's always got on well with men.'

'Even strange men?' he said quietly. 'Ones she doesn't know?'

'Jon, you're talking in riddles,' Helen protested. 'Unless you come right out and say what you mean I can't—'

'I'm saying she was as jumpy as a kitten while I was staying at her apartment, especially to start with.'

Helen stared at him again, then she slowly shook her head and said, 'Well, I'm sure I don't know what you mean. I've never known Kate like that.' She paused. 'So, what do you think it is? This nervousness. What do you think could be the reason?'

He shrugged. 'At a guess I would say she's been badly frightened at some stage.'

'I did wonder if she'd been hurt,' said Helen slowly. 'If, maybe, when she came back here it was because Alistair had ended the relationship.'

'Alistair?'

'Oh, God,' said Helen, suddenly aghast at her slip. 'Maybe I shouldn't have told you that. Please don't let on, will you?'

'Of course not. So who was he, this Alistair?'

'A lawyer. Someone she'd met in London.'

'Did you meet him?'

'Yes.' Helen nodded. 'She brought him to the Island a couple of times. Once was for Cowes Week and then, I think, one Christmas.'

'What did you think of him?'

'Well, he seemed very nice. Charming, well bred, very good-looking. But you can't really tell on such short acquaintance, can you?'

'No,' Jon agreed. 'You can't.'

Helen was silent for a moment, staring thoughtfully down at the flower border. Then she looked up. 'You don't think. . . You're not saying. . .'

'I'm not saying anything, Helen,' he replied. 'Simply observing that Kate appeared very nervous to me, and I wondered why. Call it professional speculation, if you like—'

He broke off as a car suddenly turned into the drive, and they both looked up.

'Who's this?' Helen narrowed her eyes against the bright morning sun. 'I'm not expecting anyone this morning. Don't know the car either. Oh, wait a minute. . . it's Kate!'

'Well, now,' said Jon, getting to his feet, 'there's a thing. I wonder what's brought her over here again.'

'I wonder, indeed,' said Helen drily.

Kate brought the car to a halt, switched off the engine and climbed out. Dressed in beige leggings, leather ankle boots and a russet coloured chenille sweater, her dark hair gleamed almost chestnut in the sunlight.

'Hello,' she said, her gaze flickering from Jon to Helen and back to Jon again.

'What brings you back to this neck of the woods so soon?' asked Helen.

'Special delivery,' Kate replied. 'Elizabeth French returned this car. It's the one Jon's going to use. I thought I'd bring it over so he'd have it for surgery in the morning.'

'That was very thoughtful of you,' said Jon.

'The only problem is,' said Kate, 'I'll have to ask you to run me back.'

'I can't imagine,' Helen said innocently, 'that will be a problem at all.'

A little later when Jon and Kate drove away Helen sat on the seat and watched them go. It was warm in the yard, and with a little sigh she lifted her face to the sun and closed her eyes. There was nothing quite like that first real warmth of spring sunshine, and for Helen it was always a moment to be savoured.

As the sound of the car faded into the distance Helen found herself wondering at what Jon Hammond had just told her. If what he had said was true, and that something had happened to upset Kate, surely she should have noticed—at least have been aware of it—even if Kate hadn't chosen to tell her. She was her friend, for heaven's sake. It was a pretty poor show if your best friend was so preoccupied with her own life that she failed to notice if you were upset.

Frowning slightly, Helen tried to cast her mind back to the time when Kate had first returned to the Island. She had to admit she had been surprised by Kate's return because, as she had explained to Jon, everyone had assumed Kate was all set to specialise. She had also thought that Kate was about to settle down with the man who had come into her life about that time, Alistair Cunningham.

But right out of the blue Kate had come to the Island, and the next thing anyone knew was that she was taken on as a junior partner at the Fleetwood Centre and had bought herself one of the new apartments which had just been built on Cowes seafront.

Helen tried to remember how her friend had seemed at that time, but five years is a long time and the mind can play tricks. Then, of course, shortly after Kate's arrival Diana Fleetwood had fallen ill, treatment for leukaemia had followed, albeit unsuccessfully, and her subsequent death had left devastation for them all in its wake.

After that had come her own father's illness, and for Helen there had been little time for anything else.

But if there was something wrong with Kate, something that stemmed from her time in London, it had gone unnoticed by any of them for a very long time and it had taken a newcomer, a stranger, to spot it. The ironic part was that in that stranger, for the first time for years, Helen had seen Kate's interest aroused. Whether the same interest was there for Jon Hammond Helen had no idea, but as the click of a door behind her in the house brought her out of her daydream she decided that from now on she would keep a close eye on the situation.

'Pamela? Is that you, dear? Are you there?'

With a sigh she stood up, her brief moment of respite at an end.

'I'm here, Dad,' she said, turning to go into the house. Pamela had been her mother's name.

'Last day of these cycle races today,' said Kate as Jon slowed the car behind yet another group of cyclists, all of them bent low over the handlebars of their sleek, racing machines.

'I should think it creates quite a hazard on these narrow roads,' he commented so he at last successfully overtook the group when it was safe to do.

'Yes, it does,' Kate agreed. 'But it's an annual attraction and it brings publicity to the Island, which in turn, of course, boosts tourism.'

'I wouldn't have thought that was too much of a problem,' he said, throwing her a quick glance.

'It didn't used to be,' she replied, 'not in the days of the bucket and spade family holiday, but these days with so much competition from foreign resorts we need all the publicity we can get to help the economy.'

'I suppose tourism's the major industry here?' he said a few minutes later as they approached a long hill and he dropped the car down to a lower gear.

'Yes.' Kate nodded. There are others, of course—aircraft, boatbuilding, light engineering and many rural crafts which seem to be enjoying a comeback—but tourism is still the principal one. As you will already have gathered, we also have a high population of retired people on the Island so residential and nursing homes also feature heavily in—Oh, I say, what's going on?' She broke off as, with a muttered exclamation, Jon braked sharply. They were right on the brow of the hill and the cars in front had suddenly stopped.

'Looks like there's been an accident,' said Jon, winding down his window and leaning out.

'We'd better see if we can help,' said Kate.

'I'll pull into that lay-by,' Jon replied, nodding towards the entrance to a field alongside them. 'At least that'll get us off the road.'

Seconds later they had left the car and were running up the road. At first glance it wasn't immediately apparent what had happened. A tangled mass of cycles, their wheels still spinning, was scattered across the road. A red car had slewed sideways across the road and its bonnet was wedged under a trestle table which had presumably been set up as a refreshmant point for the cyclists. Plastic cups, orange squash and bottles of mineral water were scattered over the car and on the ground.

Several people, quite obviously dazed and injured, were sitting or lying in the road. By this time other motorists had stopped and were climbing out of their vehicles.

'Has anyone called an ambulance?' shouted Kate. When no one answered she looked at Jon. 'I have my mobile in the car.'

'Right,' he said. 'You get it and I'll organise things here.'

As she darted back to her car she heard him shout to one of the motorists, instructing him to direct the traffic.

Grabbing her phone, she dialled 999, asked for Police and Ambulance Services and gave the location of the crash. That done, she hurried back to assist Jon in giving first aid to the injured.

'Three cyclists hurt, one badly,' said Jon, rapidly passing on his assessment to Kate as she joined him. 'Both the helpers behind that table have serious injuries. Driver of the car is injured. Passenger in deep shock. Can you see to the lad behind the trestle table?'

'Of course.' Kate scrambled under the table. A teenage boy was lying on the ground partly under the car. His face was very white and he appeared to be unconscious. Kate pressed her fingers to the side of his neck, feeling for a pulse. At first she thought he was dead—that he had taken the full force of the car and had been crushed to death by its sheer weight. Then her fingers felt the merest flutter of a pulse. Looking under the car, she saw he was trapped by his legs.

Crawling out again, she scrambled to the driver's side and realised that the elderly driver was slumped over the steering-wheel.

Frantically she looked round for Jon, then saw that he was kneeling on the ground beside one of the cyclists and was giving cardiac massage. She realised that the cyclist must have arrested and that there was no way she could call Jon away to assist her.

Somewhere a woman was screaming. Someone else was shouting and, even as Kate considered her next move, close by someone began to moan.

Rapidly coming to a decision, she ran round to the other side of the car. The elderly lady passenger was sitting there, staring ahead with shocked, unseeing eyes. Pulling open the door, Kate took the woman's arm.

'Come on,' she said urgently but gently. 'Let's get you out of here.'

The woman continued to stare at the top of the bank and the field beyond. Kate glanced over her shoulder and saw that one of the motorists had left his car and was running towards her.

'Give me a hand here,' she said.

'Should we move her?' asked the man doubtfully.

'I'm a doctor,' said Kate.

That seemed sufficient enough reason for the man, and he helped her to ease the woman out of the car and onto the grass verge.

'Get someone to look after her,' said Kate, after rapidly assessing that the woman appeared to have no visible injuries.

The man nodded and beckoned to his female companion who hurried over. She took off her anorak as she did so, then crouched beside the elderly lady and draped it around her shoulders.

Kate turned her attention to the driver once more, and was about to ask the man to help her again when she realised that Jon was at her side.

'The cyclist. . .?' she said, her gaze flying to the man on the ground.

'He's breathing,' said Jon. 'Let's get this one out. . .'

The driver was a big man and it took a considerable amount of effort for them to get him out of the confined space. Eventually, however, he was lying on the ground.

It was Jon who searched for the pulse this time, Jon who examined the man's pupils, then glanced up at Kate and shook his head. 'Too late for this one, I'm afraid,' he said quietly.

And moments later it was Jon who discovered the stream of petrol trickling from under the car. 'I daren't try and start the engine,' he said. 'Looks like we have a fractured fuel pipe. The whole lot could go up in flames.'

'What can we do? said Kate. 'We must get that boy out.'

'We'll have to try and push it.' Jon looked at the other

motorists who had all left their vehicles. 'Can we have some help here?' he yelled.

Within seconds he was joined by three other men, including the one who had helped Kate, and between them they managed to lift the front of the car off the injured youth. Together they pushed the car back into the centre of the road.

Kate scrambled forward again to examine the still form of the boy, and at that moment the first wailing of sirens could be heard in the distance.

The boy was bleeding heavily from a gaping wound just below his right knee. Cursing the fact that neither she nor Jon, both being off duty, had a medical bag between them, Kate looked around for something to staunch the flow of blood.

Jon, running back from the car, must have summed up the situation for he struggled out of his denim jacket and pulled off the white T-shirt he was wearing beneath. He folded the T-shirt into a firm pad and handed it down to Kate who immediately pressed it to the wound, applying just enough pressure to stop the bleeding.

At that moment the boy's eyelids fluttered open.

'It's all right, son,' said Jon kneeling beside him and smoothing the damp hair out of the boy's eyes. 'You're going to be all right now.'

Vaguely Kate had become aware of increased noise and activity behind her, and at that moment a shadow fell across them, blotting out the sun.

'Good grief!' said a voice. 'It's Dr Chapman. What're you doing here, Doc?'

Looking over her shoulder, Kate saw that an ambulance had arrived and one of the paramedics was staring down at her in amazement.

'Just happened to be passing, Dave, that's all,' she said with a wry smile.

'Thought you'd taken up cycling.'

'No chance,' Kate replied. 'Far too dangerous a sport for me.'

'Quite right, too.' Dave knelt down beside her and opened his bag. 'So, what have you got for us, Doc?' he asked, transferring his gaze to the injured boy.

It was Jon who answered. 'This lad here was crushed under the front of the car,' he said. 'Nasty leg wound. The motorist appears to have suffered a cardiac arrest. Nothing to be done there, I'm afraid. His wife is in severe shock. Of the cyclists, one has sustained serious head and chest injuries and two have minor injuries. Oh, and one lady, another of the helpers, has cuts and grazes.'

'Blimey!' The paramedic stared at him. 'So who are you? Dr Bloody Kildare?'

'Oh, Dave, sorry.' Kate looked round again. 'I should have said. This is Jon Hammond. He's our new locum. Jon, this is Dave Morey and that's his colleague, Pete Steel, over there.' She nodded towards the second paramedic who was kneeling beside the injured cyclist.

'Oh, I see.' Dave grinned. 'Pleased to meet you, Doc. I thought you were some sort of medical freak—we do get them, you know, usually at the scene of traffic accidents. Right.' He glanced around. 'Let's get this show on the road—oxygen first, don't you think?'

'We'll need more than one ambulance,' said Jon.

'There's another on the way,' Dave replied. As a police car suddenly skidded to a halt behind them he said, 'Here are the boys in blue. Better late than never, I suppose.'

Two uniformed policemen got out of the car and, adjusting their caps, walked across the road towards them.

'Beat you to it this time, lads.' With a grin Dave went back to his ambulance for oxygen and other medical equipment.

Kate and Jon continued to give what help they could as the emergency services swung into action. The police radioed for the fire service as the road required dousing, the second ambulance arrived and within a very short space of time the casualties were on their way to the Shalbrooke.

'We can take a couple in the car, if you like,' said Kate to Pete Steel.

'Yes. Fine. Thanks,' he replied. 'There are two who should go to Casualty for some treatment but whose injuries don't really warrant another ambulance.'

'You don't mind, Jon, do you?' asked Kate, turning to him.

'Not at all. Just as long as A and E don't mind me being shirtless.'

'I'm sure they've seen worse,' said Kate, her eyes automatically drawn to the smooth bronzed skin visible beneath his denim jacket.

Leaving the police to organise the removal of the damaged cycles, Kate and Jon, together with two of the less injured cyclists, got back into their car and followed the ambulances as, with blue lights flashing and sirens wailing, they headed for the Shalbrooke. They had travelled barely a mile when they passed a fire engine racing towards the scene of the accident.

Their passengers turned out to be a young man and his girlfriend who had come to the Island specifically for the racing. They both appeared to be in shock and spoke very little *en route* to the hospital. The man had received a blow on the head when he had been knocked from his cycle and looked as if he might be suffering from mild concussion, while his girlfriend had lacerations to her legs and grazes to one elbow and to the side of her face.

When they reached the Shalbrooke Kate told Jon to drive straight into the parking bay for Accident and Emergency rather than park in the main car park. 'I know it's Sunday,' she said, 'but A and E can still get very busy.'

Her words were borne out as, together with their passengers, they entered Reception and it appeared just as crowded as it did on any weekday. As they approached the desk Kate saw that Georgina Merrick was on duty.

'Hello, Georgina,' she said. 'Two more patients for you here—victims of the RTA.'

'Hello, Kate.' Georgina looked as surprised to see her as Dave Morey had been.

'We're just doing our good deed for the day,' Kate said. Turning to Jon, she added, 'This is Jon Hammond, by the way—Paul's locum. Jon, Georgina Merrick.'

The staff nurse had been about to turn her attention to the patients but she stopped and threw Jon a quick, keen glance.

'Oh,' she said, 'so you're Jon Hammond. 'I've been hearing a lot about you.' Her gaze flickered to Kate, and Kate found herself wondering just what she had heard. 'I understand,' Georgina went on, 'that you're staying in Helen Turner's flat?'

'News travels fast—I only moved in yesterday.' Jon smiled, his easy, laid-back smile as he held out his hand. 'And you're Georgina Merrick. I've been hearing a lot about you as well.'

'Really?' Georgina looked amazed. 'Whatever have you been hearing about me?'

'That you're about to marry your ex-husband.'

'Oh, that. Yes.' Georgina flushed.

'I think it's really neat,' said Jon. 'I never knew anyone do that before.'

Kate smiled. Then, the roadcrash victims no longer their responsibility, she and Jon made their way out of Reception. They passed Dave Morey and Pete Steel in the parking bay as the two paramedics were returning the stretchers and blankets to their ambulance.

'Thanks for your help,' called Dave.

'It's a pleasure,' said Jon, while Kate raised her hand and smiled.

For some inexplicable reason, she felt extraordinarily good as they got back into the car. She wasn't sure why, but as she stole a glance at the man at her side she had the feeling that working alongside him in a highly charged situation might have had something to do with the way she felt.

He drove her home, drawing the car to a halt on the seafront before her apartment and switching off the engine. Suddenly she felt at a loss for words and found herself desperately searching for something to say.

'Did you miss me?' he said, glancing up at the apartment.

'I beg your pardon?' It took her so by surprise that she stared at him in astonishment.

'Last night. Was it quiet without me?' he said.

'Well.' She took a deep breath. 'It seemed a little strange, I have to admit. I'd got quite used to having you...to having someone around the place.' She corrected herself hastily, not wanting him to get the wrong impression. Before he could ask another compromising question she said quickly, 'Are you comfortable at Helen's?'

'Oh, yes,' he replied casually. 'It's fine.' He paused. 'Although, I have to say—'

'Yes,' she said quickly. 'What?'

'Somehow there's something missing.'

'Oh, really?' she replied, equally casual. Then, before he could elaborate, she added, 'I dare say it was the sea.'

'The sea?' He turned his head to look at her and she couldn't help but notice the quizzical amusement in his eyes.

'Yes,' she replied briskly as she opened the car door, 'one gets used to the sound of the sea very quickly, almost subconsciously. When it's no longer there it leaves an emptiness,' she concluded as she climbed out of the car.

'Is that so?' He leaned across the seat as she closed the door and looked at her through the open window. 'I'll remember that. When I feel that empty feeling in future I'll know what causes it.'

He smiled just before he drove away and Kate had the distinct impression that he was mocking her, but as she stood and watched the car disappear from her view she found that, far from dreading the thought of him starting work at the centre the next morning as she had previously, she was now actually looking forward to having him about the place.

There was certainly something about the man, she was forced to admit as she turned to go indoors with a sigh. It seemed that the more she got to know him the more surprised she became that her initial impression of him had been so way off the mark.

CHAPTER SEVEN

JON'S car was already there when Kate arrived. In Reception there seemed a buzz, an alertness about the girls not usually in evidence on an average Monday morning.

'Good morning, Dr Chapman.' Claire seemed pink and a little breathless.

'Morning, Claire.' Kate eyed the receptionist warily. Claire had a reputation for getting a bit over-excited at times.

'Dr Hammond's here,' Claire breathed reverently.

'Good,' observed Kate.

'He's in Dr Wooldridge's room. I've just taken him the post and a coffee.'

'I'm surprised he hasn't got you calling him by his first name,' said Kate tartly as she picked up her own pile of post from the desk and leafed through the envelopes.

'Oh, he did say we could,' said Claire solemnly.

Kate threw her a sharp glance.

'But it wouldn't be right, would it, Dr Chapman? I mean, we don't do that, do we, not in surgery?'

'No, Claire,' Kate agreed, 'we don't.'

'It's different out of surgery, of course,' said Claire, 'as Dr Hammond pointed out. So socially I shall call him Jon,' she added dreamily.

Taking a deep breath, Kate took herself off to her room.

She'd only been there a few minutes—just long enough to take off her jacket, turn on her computer and sit down at her desk—when Elizabeth French tapped on her door and came into the room.

'Hello.' Kate smiled. 'I hear he's installed, then? Our new recruit.'

'Oh, yes,' Elizabeth replied softly. 'Very much so. He certainly seems to have made himself at home. Has the girls eating out of his hand.'

'So I gather,' said Kate drily. 'No one's brought me coffee yet.'

Eliazabeth laughed. 'You don't have blond hair or a lean, hungry look and you happen to be the wrong sex.'

'What's he wearing?' Kate looked up suddenly.

'Wearing?' Elizabeth frowned.

'Yes. He went to buy some new clothes—thank heavens.' Kate gave a little shudder. 'The thought of him taking surgery in his bush gear. . .'

'Oh, he's bought new clothes, all right,' said Elizabeth.

'I'm glad to hear it,' Kate replied, trying to imagine him in a plain grey suit, a crisp white shirt and a tie and failing miserably. Not that the idea wasn't without its appeal. Somehow the thought of Jon Hammond in formal dress, unlikely as it was, was curiously stimulating—those broad shoulders in a well-fitting suit, the dazzling white of a shirt against the sun-bleached hair and brown skin. . .the distant look in those grey eyes. . .

She dismissed the disturbing thoughts as she realised that Elizabeth had changed the subject and had started to discuss some blood-test results which had arrived in the morning mail. Even then she found it difficult to concentrate, and the situation got little better as the morning wore on and she began to see her patients.

She found it almost impossible to get him out of her mind. All she could think about was the fact that he was here in the building, only a stone's throw away, sitting in Paul's room, at Paul's desk, seeing Paul's patients.

Her irrational thoughts only added to the confusion she already felt after the events of the last few days—missing him after he'd moved out of her flat, the strange, totally unreasonable feelings, almost of jealousy, of him staying in Helen's flat and then the curious elation she had experienced after they had worked together at the scene of the previous day's road accident.

And now here she was in her consulting room, seeing one patient after another, on what was a perfectly normal Monday morning, and all she could do was think how good it felt that he was in the same building.

Anyone would think she was falling for the man. Which, of course, was utterly ridiculous. That was the last thing she would allow to happen. They were poles apart and, after all, what would be the point?

Just supposing she was to get involved—have a relationship with him, learn to care for someone again— only to have him disappear out of her life and go back to Africa, as he undoubtedly would when Paul returned. Could she cope with that? She'd almost gone under the last time after Alistair. But that was different, she told herself firmly.

Jon Hammond was not Alistair.

But that didn't mean she might not learn to care for him as much as she had for Alistair. It didn't mean she wouldn't be as devastated when it ended, whatever the reason.

On the other hand, what gave her reason to suppose that he might be even remotely interested in her? Had he given any indication that was? The meal he'd prepared for her? Probably just gratitude. The way he sometimes looked at her with that quizzical half-smile? He, no doubt, did that to every female. Claire was quite obviously smitten, was probably sitting in Reception at that moment, having the same sort of thoughts as herself and desperately trying to think of some excuse for going down the corridor to Paul Wooldridge's consulting room.

So lost in her thoughts had Kate become that she jumped violently as her phone suddenly rang.

'Dr Chapman?' It was Jackie. 'Did you know you have three more patients waiting?'

'What? Oh, yes. Yes, of course,' said Kate.

'Oh, sorry,' said Jackie. 'It's just that we wondered, seeing you haven't buzzed for anyone for the last quarter of an hour.'

'You can send the next one in now, Jackie,' she said crisply.

'Yes, Dr Chapman. But before I do I have Helen Turner on the other line. She wants to know if she can have a quick word with you.'

'Yes, of course. Put her through.' She waited.

'Hello, Kate. Sorry to bother you,' said Helen. 'Have you finished surgery?'

'Not quite. I'm running a bit late.'

'Oh, I'm sorry. I thought you would be finished. Would you like me to ring back?'

'No, Helen,' she replied wearily. 'It's OK. I just don't seem to be able to get my act together this morning, that's all.'

'Well, I won't keep you a moment. I was just ringing to ask whether you would like to come to the party we're giving for Georgina and Andrew Merrick after their wedding on Saturday.'

'That's kind of you, Helen. I should love to. Thank

you. I saw Georgina yesterday when I was in A and E. I must say she looks very happy.'

'She said she saw you,' Helen replied. 'And, yes, she is very happy. I gather you and Jon were quite involved with the RTA?'

'Yes, we were,' Kate agreed. 'It was one of those "in the right place at the right time" incidents. Speaking of which, have you heard anything about the young man who was trapped under the car?'

'He was all right, apparently, apart from a couple of fractures.' Helen paused. 'Unfortunately, the cyclist didn't make it.'

'Oh, dear. Does Jon know that?'

'No, I only heard myself when I came in this morning.'

'He arrested just after the accident,' said Kate. 'Jon resuscitated him.'

'According to Andrew Merrick, he arrested twice more soon after arrival in A and E. The second time they couldn't revive him. Perhaps you'd tell Jon. How's he getting on, by the way?' Helen added, as if as an afterthought.

'I don't know,' Kate admitted. 'I haven't seen him yet this morning. But I should imagine if he's charmed the patients as much as he has the receptionists he'll be doing just fine.'

Helen laughed. 'He's a nice guy,' she said. 'I could be charmed myself.'

'I doubt Richard would approve of that.'

'Probably not. But it might make him appreciate me a bit more. Kate, this is all very well but I must go, and I must let you get on. I can count on you for Saturday night, then? We need to have some idea of numbers.'

'Yes, of course. I'll be there.'

She hung up and was about to press the buzzer for her next patient when, on a sudden impulse, she stood up, crossed her room, tugged open the door and strode purposefully down the corridor to Paul Wooldridge's consulting room.

She tapped on the door and entered the room, barely waiting for his call.

He was sitting behind the desk, but his chair was facing the window and he was gazing out at the fields behind the centre. He swivelled round to face her, and very briefly she caught some emotion in his eyes. She wasn't certain what it was, but it could almost have been pleasure.

'Kate. I thought they'd found another patient for me.'

'No, it's only me. . . I've just spoken to Helen. . .I thought you might want to know. . .' She trailed off as she caught sight of what he was wearing.

'Is there anything wrong?' A hint of amusement entered his eyes.

'Oh, no,' she said hastily, 'it's just that. . . Oh, nothing.' She had been prepared to find him wearing new clothes— Elizabeth had said he was wearing them. What she hadn't been prepared for was that they should be a new pair of jeans and a dark green collarless shirt over a fresh white T-shirt.

'You were expecting me to be wearing a collar and tie and a pressed grey suit, weren't you?' he said as he read her mind with uncanny precision.

'No, of course not—'

'Yes, you were. Go on, admit it.'

'Well, I. . .' She floundered, trying to find the right thing to say. Something that wouldn't give too much offence.

'Sorry, Kate.' He grinned. 'I'm not a suit man, and I

never will be. Besides, what would I do with a suit when I go back to Tanzania?'

The sudden mention of his eventual return to Africa caused Kate a pang of desolation. She swallowed. 'Jon, listen, what I came to tell you was that Helen said the cyclist yesterday—he didn't make it, I'm afraid. He arrested twice more, apparently, and the second time he couldn't be revived.'

'I'm not really surprised.' Jon's expression had grown serious. 'His injuries were pretty horrific. I guess he caught the full impact of the car.' He paused. 'Have you finished your surgery?' he asked.

Kate shook her head. 'Not quite. How did your first surgery go?'

'Pretty well, really. Once folk had got over the initial shock I think they seemed to quite like me—at least, most of them went away happily enough. One or two seemed a bit bemused by my approach.' He gave a wry smile, then added, 'I understand we have a staff meeting at lunchtime.'

'Heavens,' said Kate, 'I'd forgotten that. I'd better get finished. Richard gets twitchy if anyone's late for a meeting.' She turned to go.

'Oh, Kate.' Jon called her back.

'Yes?'

'Did Helen say anything to you about Saturday night?'

She frowned, not understanding for a moment which Saturday he was referring to.

'She said she was going to,' he went on, 'when she asked me about it this morning. I must say it sounds as if it could be fun.'

'You mean the party for Georgina and Andrew?' she asked in surprise.

'Of course. What did you think I meant?' He raised quizzical eyebrows.

'I don't know. Oh, nothing.' Suddenly she felt puzzled. She could understand Helen inviting her to the party. After all, she'd known both Georgina and Andrew Merrick for a long time. But it seemed strange that she should ask Jon Hammond.

For the second time that morning he appeared to read her thoughts.

'I thought it kind of Helen to ask me. She said it would be a good opportunity for me to meet people.'

'Well, yes. It will be, of course.' Suddenly she felt pleased, ridiculously pleased that he was going. She didn't want him to know that, however, so, with a muttered excuse to the effect that she really must finish her surgery, she finally hurried out of his room.

She was the last to arrive at the staff meeting, earning a look from Richard Fleetwood who was in the chair.

'Sorry, Richard,' she said, and took her place at the table between Martin Hogan and Kay Selby, one of the practice nurses.

'Right,' said Richard, 'now that Kate is here we'll get started. General meeting first, with practice business followed by a case history.' He glanced round at the others who nodded in agreement, before turning their attention to the agenda.

Glancing up, Kate realised that Jon was seated directly opposite her. He must have sensed her eyes on him for he, too, looked up, his gaze meeting hers. Quickly she looked away.

'First and foremost,' said Richard, 'I would like to formally welcome Jon Hammond to the practice. I know you will do all you can to make his time here as pleasant as possible. Jon. . .' he turned to the locum '. . .I hope you'll be happy with us.'

'Thanks.' Jon inclined his head. 'I'm sure I will be.'

'I understand,' said Richard, 'that your accommodation is sorted out?'

'Thanks to Kate.' Jon looked at her, and as everyone else followed suit Kate felt her cheeks redden.

'It was no problem,' she muttered. 'It was all down to Helen Turner, really.'

'And you have the practice car to use,' Richard went on. When Jon nodded in response he said, 'You will basically take over Paul's list. He did, however, take a rather larger than usual number of extra clinics. The rest of us have agreed we'll assist with that particular work-load. It wouldn't be reasonable to expect you to cope with all that when you aren't even familiar with the area, let alone the patients. The other thing, of course, is that we shall soon be moving into the season, which brings with it the inevitable increase in temporary residents. We tend to share those between us. Do you have any objections to that, Jon?'

'Of course not. I'm happy to help out wherever I can,' said Jon.' He paused. 'I have to say, though, there is one area that is giving me a few nightmares.'

Kate looked up sharply, wondering what he was about to say.

'Oh?' said Richard. 'What's that?'

'Well,' said Jon slowly, 'in Tanzania, there weren't too many computers.'

'How many, Jon?' asked Martin Hogan with a laugh.

'Now that you ask, I don't ever remember seeing one,'

admitted Jon. 'The thing is, I have to confess I haven't a clue how to use them.'

'I shouldn't worry too much, if I were you, Jon,' said Elizabeth French suddenly. 'There are still a few people around here who don't have much idea how to use them either.'

Amidst the general laughter around the table, Richard said, 'That's probably very true but at least we've had them installed for some time now whereas as Jon says, he's completely unfamiliar with them. Is there anyone who would be willing to show him the basics just so that he at least is able to use one during surgery?'

'I will,' Kate heard herself say.

'Very well, Kate, thanks,' said Richard. 'So it's welcome aboard, Jon. Now...' He paused and looked down at his notes '...we have a lot to get through so if we could move on, please. I have some general information regarding fund-holding that I need to give you...'

Kate glanced up and found that Jon was looking at her again.

'Thanks.' He mouthed the word and she flushed slightly and smiled in embarrassment. She didn't know what had prompted her to say she would help him with the computer. It had taken her long enough to learn, as it was, and she still wasn't completely comfortable with it. Besides, wasn't her workload heavy enough, without adding to it unnecessarily?

The agenda moved from fund-holding to the allocation of appointments—a topic which never seemed to be satisfactorily resolved—then on to staff hours and Richard's work at the Shalbrooke where he stood in as a locum anaesthetist, followed by a discussion on the new proposals for night visits.

'I can't see it working, myself,' said Martin gloomily. 'Two doctors on call for the whole Island, you say?'

Richard nodded. 'But they will be centrally based on site, messages will be taken through ambulance control and each doctor will have a driver with a highly powered vehicle fitted with a warning system.'

'Huh!' Martin looked far from convinced.

'What area is the Island?' It was Jon who spoke, and everyone looked at him as he made his first contribution to the meeting.

'It's twenty-two miles across at the furthest points,' said Martin, 'and it covers about a hundred and fifty square miles—that's quite an area.'

'A bit less than the distances you are used to in the bush, Jon,' said Kate with a slight smile, remembering the story he had told her about the women and how far they would walk, either for water or with a sick child.

'That's an entirely different matter,' said Martin. 'All due respects, Jon, but your people don't know any different. People in this country have been used to having a doctor at their beck and call at all hours of the day or night.'

'They still will,' said Kay Selby.

'They won't like it,' muttered Martin.

'Well, time will tell,' replied Richard. 'We'll never know if these things are successful unless they are tried.'

'Well, I for one won't be sorry at not having to go out alone at night any more,' said Kate. Her remark was met with murmurs of agreement.

'I can't imagine the crime rate being too high here,' said Jon, looking around the table.

'It isn't, particularly,' Kate replied, 'and at one time it never bothered me, but I have to admit that recently there have been occasions when I've felt threatened.'

'Would that have happened to you, Jon?' asked Elizabeth. 'In the bush, I mean. Did you ever feel threatened?'

'Oh, yes,' he said, 'but not quite in the way you mean.' When the others all looked at him with interest he went on, 'Our danger would have come from a charging rhino or a hungry lion, rather than from drug-crazed humans. Crime was practically unheard of around the bush station. The people are very contented with their lot but their principles are high and discipline is always maintained. As civilisation creeps in, however, together with Western cultures, their expectations change and they become aware of alternative lifestyles. That's when the trouble starts.'

Everyone was silent for a moment, as if reflecting on what Jon had said, then Kay, who was of West Indian origin, said, 'Will you go back, Dr Hammond?'

'Oh, yes,' he replied. 'It's been nice to return to the old country, but I guess my heart's still in Africa.'

Kate swallowed as Richard cleared his throat and said, 'Well, that just about concludes the business side of the meeting for today. We have a case history to discuss next which, I think, everyone needs to be aware of. It concerns the Everton family who are actually registered with Paul so that means, Jon. . .' he threw the locum a quick glance '. . .that you will most probably become involved. In the last few weeks I think we have all at some time or the other seen one of this family, either in surgery or on a house call. Kate, I believe you were the most recent one to be involved. Would you care to outline the case to put Jon in the picture and to bring the rest of us up to date?'

Kate opened the folder that Elizabeth French passed to her.

'The Everton family,' she began, 'consists of seven members—father, mother and five children, ranging from two years to seventeen years. Denis Everton has worked only intermittently as a labourer and has served two terms in prison. He is currently serving time for burglary. Marion Everton has an alcohol problem. After the birth of her last child she received treatment and, we believe, managed to stay off the drink. Since her husband's conviction, however, she has been drinking again. The oldest child, a girl, recently had a baby and sometimes lives at home, sometimes with her boyfriend. The two older boys, aged twelve and fourteen, are constantly in trouble with the juvenile courts, and the younger children have been placed on the at risk register.'

'Is there a history of violence?' asked Jon.

Kate shook her head. 'Not as far as we know. The risk comes from neglect, most likely as a result of the mother's drinking.'

'So what is the current position?'

'Social Services are keeping a close eye on the situation,' replied Richard, 'but I feel we all need to be aware of what is happening.'

There were nods of agreement from the others, and as Richard drew the meeting to a close papers and folders were collected, chairs pushed back and the staff began to file out of the room.

'Thanks for offering to help me with the computer,' said Jon.

Kate threw him a quick glance and saw that he was still sitting at the table, toying with a pencil.

'That's OK,' she replied. 'We should have thought of it before. It never occurred to me that you wouldn't be familiar with them. It obviously had never occurred to any of the others either.'

Jon looked over his shoulder and, seeing that they were the only two left in the room, said, 'Tell me, is Martin always such a prophet of doom?'

Kate laughed. 'Not really. He just comes over that way sometimes.'

'He sounded as if he actually enjoyed night visits.'

'Maybe he does,' Kate replied with a wry laugh.

'I can't understand how anyone could actually enjoy being pulled out of bed in the middle of the night and forced to leave the house. . .'

'You haven't met his wife, Patsy,' said Kate darkly. As Jon looked at her in astonishment she gave a peal of laughter and clapped her hand over her mouth. 'You didn't hear that,' she said. 'In fact, if I'm questioned I'll deny I ever said it.'

Amusement entered Jon's eyes. 'I keep hearing veiled references to Patsy,' he said. 'Is she really that bad?'

'You'll probably meet her at the party on Saturday,' Kate replied. 'You'll be able to judge for yourself.'

He stood up. 'Well, I can't say I haven't been warned. Now, when are you going to be able to spare the time to show me this computer?'

Kate looked at her watch. 'They say there's no time like the present so how about now? It'll mean my missing lunch—but what's a mere thing like a missed lunch between friends?'

'What, indeed?' said Jon softly as he followed her from the staffroom.

CHAPTER EIGHT

'YOU'LL have to start right at the beginning,' said Jon. 'Like I said, I know nothing at all about these things.'

'Well,' said Kate, entering her password and waiting as the 'Welcome' sign appeared on the screen, 'I take it you understand the basic principles?'

'Remind me.' He was sitting beside her very close, and as he leaned forward to study the screen he moved even closer.

'It's just a big storage machine, really, to file things or—put another way—it's a memory.'

'A bit like a human brain, I suppose.'

'Yes,' Kate agreed, 'but less unpredictable. A brain can forget things but a computer doesn't. The main thing, though, is to understand that it is only like a brain in that it remembers—it can't, of course, think for itself and it only retains what is put into it in the first place.'

'I have heard horror stories about these things crashing and losing everything,' he said solemnly.

'That does happen sometimes,' said Kate, 'which is why we back up everything that we store on the hard disk onto floppy disks so that if it did crash we wouldn't lose anything.'

'What was that word that you put in a moment ago?'

'That was my password,' she replied. 'We each have our own password that opens the system—a bit like a key, really.'

'This is a central system?'

'Yes.'

'So are you saying that I could send messages to you via the screen from the computer in my room?'

'That's right, yes.'

'Amazing,' he said.

She threw him a quick glance. Suddenly she had the feeling he was having her on, that really he knew exactly what she was telling him and he was just seeing how far he could make her go.

His face was expressionless, however, and he was staring intently at the screen. 'What exactly do we have in the memory?' he asked a moment later.

'The girls have loaded a tremendous amount of data into the system,' she explained. 'Details of every patient registered with the practice are there—name, address, age, occupation, medication and brief details of illnesses and operations. So if, for example, a patient comes to you with a complaint they had, say, two years ago you can call up their medication chart—like this. . .' She pressed severa keys to illustrate what she meant. 'Then you can see what was prescribed for them on that occasion. If it was successful and you wish to repeat that medication you can then ask the computer to print a prescription.'

'Well,' said Jon as he watched the printer, 'I'm impressed.'

'What would your friends in the bush make of that?' Kate laughed as she tore off the specimen prescription and handed it to him for his approval.

'I'm not too sure,' he replied. 'I think they might suspect witchcraft.'

'What is their religion?' asked Kate suddenly fascinated again by what he was telling her.

'Christianity for the most part,' he said. 'The mission

was set up first and we moved in afterwards, as is so often the case, but the old superstitions still linger, especially in the more remote bush areas.'

'Well, I don't think you'll get much magic out of this thing.' Kate smiled. 'What it does may be clever, but I wouldn't call it magic by any stretch of the imagination. Now, let me show you how we recall patients for certain types of testing.'

He leaned forward again, so close now that his arm brushed hers. Her first inclination was to pull away, but as she realised how petty it would seem she resisted and they remained close.

'What sort of testing did you mean?' he asked, staring intently at the screen again as if he was trying to retain everything she was saying and storing it in his own memory for future use.

'Well, for example, supposing we wanted to test all ten-year-old girls for rubella. We could ask the computer to select every ten-year-old female who is registered with us. We could then individually check their records and send out appointments or reminders to those who hadn't had rubella and who needed a vaccination.'

'Incredible!' He moved away and, leaning back in his chair, linked his hands behind his head.

Again Kate had the fleeting impression that, really, he had known all along, but it disappeared as he said, 'Would you watch now while I have a go?'

'Of course.'

He seemed to grasp the basic principles very quickly so it was with a certain amount of surprise when at the end Kate heard him say, 'It's going to take me some time, I think, to really get the hang of all this. Do you think you could spare the time if I were to come in, say, each morning before we start or, if you prefer, in the evenings when we've finished—at least for this week?' He paused and looked up her, his expression rueful yet at the same time boyishly appealing. 'Or would that be presuming on your good nature too much?'

'Oh,' she said, 'no. No, of course not.'

What else could she have said? she asked herself later. She could hardly have refused, having offered to help him in the first place. Not that she was certain she wanted to refuse, anyway. And as the week passed, surprisingly quickly it seemed, she found herself reflecting on more than one occasion how nice it was to have him around. She'd liked the previous locum, Simon Phillips. He, too, had been friendly, sociable and good at his job, but he hadn't been like Jon Hammond. If she'd been asked to pinpoint the difference Kate would have been hard put to say why.

There was something about Jon Hammond that was exciting. Yes, that was it, she told herself as she sat in her consulting room one afternoon, once again trying to analyse her feelings—exciting, and slightly outrageous as if there were some force of energy pent-up inside him, just straining for release.

Her earlier fears that she might have been falling in love with the man had been completely misplaced, of course, but that didn't alter the fact that as the Easter weekend crept closer she realised she was looking forward to the party at the hospital, and the prime reason for that was quite simply because Jon Hammond was going to be there.

The social club at the Shalbrooke had been specially decorated with fresh spring flowers, streamers and helium-filled balloons for the party to celebrate the remarriage of two of the hospital's most popular members of staff. A huge banner over the raised platform proclaimed congratulations to the happy couple who stood at the entrance to welcome their guests.

'Kate, how good of you to come.' Andrew Merrick kissed her cheek.

'I wouldn't have missed it for the world.' Kate turned to kiss Georgina. 'You look gorgeous,' she said. 'What a wonderful colour that is.'

'Thank you.' Georgina laughed. 'The girls wanted me to wear white, but I thought that was pushing things a bit too far so I settled for this.' She glanced down as she spoke at the creamy-gold silk dress she was wearing.

'How did the ceremony go?'

'It was lovely,' said Georgina softly with a quick look at Andrew. 'Very quiet, just our families and a couple of very close friends.'

'At the registry office?' asked Kate.

'Yes.' It was Andrew who answered. 'Followed by a renewal of our vows at the church where we were married. It seemed only right and the vicar was only too delighted to oblige.'

'I think that's wonderful,' said Kate, suddenly having to swallow a lump that had risen in her throat.

Andrew smiled. 'We thought we were going to get away with just the quiet family lunch afterwards at our favourite hotel, but the staff had other ideas.'

'Quite right, too.' As others arrived behind her Kate began to move on into the club. 'Everyone wants to share your happiness and show how pleased they are for you both,' she added.

'Thanks,' said Georgina.

'Enjoy yourself,' called Andrew.

Kate paused for a moment, gazing round at the decor-
ations and at the same time adjusting her eyes to the
slightly dimmed lights inside the club. A disco had been
set up on the platform, complete with strobe lighting,
while catering staff were loading large tables that ran the
entire length of one wall. She had thought she was early,
that she would be one of the first to arrive, but already
the bar area was thronged with staff and guests and the
small individual tables around the edges of the dance floor
were becoming crowded.

'Kate!' She turned as she heard her name called. 'Kate,
over here!'

It was Helen, beckoning frantically to her from the far
end of the club.

She made her way down the long room and saw that
there was quite a crowd around Helen's table.

'We saved you a place,' said Helen.

Kate noticed her friend was wearing a blue top and a
long skirt in black velvet and had drawn back her ash-
blonde hair and fastened it with a black bow. The effect
was understated yet elegant. Richard Fleetwood was sitting beside her, and as Kate turned to greet him she
suddenly realised that the person sitting on Richard's other
side, who had been partly obscured by him, was Jon
Hammond.

She hadn't thought he had arrived yet, and at her first
sight of him, coming so totally unexpectedly as it did, her
heart suddenly turned over. Goodness knows why, she
thought helplessly, Richard totally forgotten as Jon stood
up and she found herself gazing into those steady
grey eyes.

She hadn't seen him that day, a day that had dragged

on and on, but she'd seen him only the day before and every day for the past week so what could be the reason for the erratic thumping of her heart now?

'Kate,' he said, 'you look lovely.' He said it not so much as a compliment but more as a statement of fact, something that wasn't open to opinion or conjecture.

'Thank you,' she murmured, moving forward and taking the chair beside him. She had dressed with great care. She'd examined the entire contents of her wardrobe during the afternoon, trying on every garment and rejecting everything, then in desperation she'd driven to Yarmouth to her favourite dress shop and thrown herself on the mercy of the salesperson. 'I need something very special,' she'd said. 'I need it for tonight. Something formal yet not, something smart yet casual—no power dressing, something soft and feminine.'

'I have just the thing,' the voice of years of experience replied.

And she had, too. It was one of those occasions, which happened all too rarely, when Kate knew she looked just right. Her outfit was black harem pants in the softest chiffon shot with silver thread, worn with a matching bolero and a cream satin shirt with huge sleeves gathered tightly at the wrists.

As Jon gazed at her in admiration Kate realised that tonight he also looked different. For once the jeans had been replaced by black trousers and a royal blue shirt. Fleetingly she wondered if these clothes had been lurking in the depths of one of the canvas holdalls or whether he also had bought something new for the evening.

'Kate, what would you like to drink?' Richard was speaking, and as she turned to look at him she saw a hint of amusement in his eyes, as if he was summing up a situation and coming to inevitable conclusions.

'Oh, a St Clements, please,' she said as she took her place beside Jon.

'I was just thinking,' he observed as Richard took himself off to the bar, that those guys running the disco look familiar. . .'

'They should do.' Kate chuckled. That's Dave Morey and Pete Steel, the two paramedics who came to the RTA last weekend.'

'Obviously men of many talents,' Jon observed. 'Either that or a spot of moonlighting.'

'Not even that.' It was Helen who replied, having overheard Jon's remark. 'All their proceeds from disco work go towards an appeal for a kidney dialysis machine.'

'Nice one.' Jon nodded, took a mouthful of his drink and glanced round the rapidly filling club. 'Who are the girls?' he asked after a moment.

Kate looked over her shoulder. 'Oh, that's Lauren and Natasha,' she said, 'Georgina's and Andrew's daughters.'

'Two very happy little girls tonight,' said Helen. Standing up, she added, 'I'll go and help Richard with the drinks.'

'Would you like me to go?' said Jon.

'Oh, no,' said Helen quickly. 'You stay and talk to Kate.'

There was an awkward little silence as Helen left the table then they both started to talk at the same time.

'Sorry,' said Kate. 'After you.'

'No. Go on, please,' said Jon.

'I was only going to say that Lauren, especially, was terribly upset at the time of her parents' divorce.'

'How old was she?'

'Well, let's see, now.' Kate considered. 'She's about

ten now so when they split up she could only have been about seven or eight—not a good age.'

'I'm not sure any age is right,' he said.

She threw him a quick glance and saw that his face was set. 'You said that as if you knew.'

'I do,' he replied tightly. 'I was twelve when my parents parted but it was arguably the biggest trauma of my life.'

She stared at him, remembering what he'd said about his mother living in Newbury but that he'd been convalescing with friends in Norfolk. She'd wondered about that at the time. Now she wondered even more.

'Who did you go with?' she asked after a moment. 'Which parent, I mean?'

'They had joint custody,' he replied, 'which at the time seemed like a good idea. I suppose it could have been in that I should have had the best of both worlds.'

'But it wasn't like that at all?' she prompted. 'Is that what you're saying?'

'I guess so. In retrospect I suppose it would have been better if I'd stayed with one or the other. As it was, I was shunted backwards and forwards like a parcel, and in the end I never felt I fitted in with either family. They both remarried and had more children. They did their best, I know, but I was always the odd one out—never felt I truly belonged anywhere.'

'That's really sad,' said Kate. And she meant it. It was sad but at the same time it explained so much. The possible reason why he was such a loner. The fact that he had no real roots. The type of lifestyle he'd adopted for himself.

'Looks like there's a happier ending for those two.' He nodded towards Lauren and Natasha who, in the cream dresses and burgundy sashes they'd worn for the ceremony, were talking and laughing with friends and relatives. Andrew and Georgina joined them at that moment and they took their places at a table. 'Why did they split up?' Jon asked after a moment.

'He had an affair,' Kate replied briefly. 'Georgina was devastated. She filed for divorce. The divorce went through, but just recently she went back to her old job on A and E. Helen swears that working together again made them realise how much they still loved each other.'

'Makes a change to hear something like that,' Jon said. 'If only more couples could try to resolve their differences, instead of imagining that one single crisis heralds the end of a marriage.'

'It's not always that simple.' Kate spoke more sharply than she'd intended, and Jon threw her a surprised glance. 'What I mean,' she added, seeing his expression, 'is that some situations are intolerable to live with—you should hear some of the stories that I'm told at my women's clinics.'

'I can imagine,' he said wryly. 'But it would be interesting to know the statistics for the proportion of marriages that break up because of those truly intolerable reasons.'

When Kate remained silent he said, 'So what, to you, would constitute a truly intolerable situation?'

'Violence.' Her reply was so instantaneous that again he shot her a glance. 'Yes,' she added more slowly, 'definitely violence, either to the partner or to any children.'

'Anything else?' Just for one moment she thought she detected a slight hint of amusement in his grey eyes, in the raised eyebrows, then it was gone and she decided she must have imagined it.

'Persistent infidelity, I suppose. . .'

'Only persistent? A one-off would be OK?'

'What?' She stared at him. 'Oh, I don't know,' she replied impatiently as she suddenly realised that this time he really was laughing at her. 'What is this, the Spanish Inquisition?'

'Sorry.' Still laughing, he glanced up as Richard and Helen returned to the table with their drinks. By this time some couples, encouraged by the good-natured banter from Dave Morey, had taken to the dance floor.

As Helen and Richard took their places at the table again they were all distracted by loud shrieks of laughter from the far side of the room.

'Oh, God,' said Richard, without turning round. 'I'd know that sound anywhere. Please tell me they aren't coming over here.'

'Can't do that, I'm afraid,' said Helen lightly. 'They've seen us and are making their way across.'

'Oh, no,' groaned Richard. Glancing at Jon, he said, 'You haven't had this particular pleasure yet, have you, Jon?'

'Which pleasure is that?' asked Jon, rising to his feet as Martin Hogan, together with a plump, dark-haired woman, stopped in front of their table.

'Of making the acquaintance of Martin's wife,' murmured Richard out of the side of his mouth. 'Martin, hello.' Richard turned to his partner. 'We were just saying that Jon hasn't yet met Patsy.'

Introductions and further greetings were carried out, followed by the unavoidable invitation for the Hogans to join them.

Ten minutes later Jon took Kate's hand and drew her onto the dance floor.

'I wouldn't have taken you for a dancing man,' she murmured into his ear.

'I'm not usually,' he replied, 'but these are exceptional circumstances. Is she always like that?'

'Afraid so.'

'But she never pauses for breath. She never stops talking.'

'Only to laugh.'

'Poor Martin. How does he put up with it?'

'He loves her,' Kate replied simply.

'He must do.'

'Actually,' Kate said with a chuckle, 'she's a very warm-hearted soul.'

'I'm sure she is,' Jon replied grimly, 'and I don't mean any disrespect but I doubt whether I could put up with that for too long.'

'So, would that constitute one of your personal reasons for divorce?' asked Kate lightly.

He laughed and drew her closer. 'It very probably could.' He was silent for a moment as they swayed to the music. Then he said, 'Are we stuck with them now? Do we have to put up with that for the rest of the evening?'

'It looks like it,' said Kate.

'I'm not sure I can stand it.'

'The only answer is to stay on the dance floor.'

'I guess you're right. What will Richard and Helen do?'

'They're already on the floor,' replied Kate, standing on tiptoe and looking over his shoulder to where she could see Helen's fair head against the darkness of Richard's jacket. 'And poor Helen will have to stay until the end, seeing she's organised this.'

'You mean the likes of us could sneak away?'

'I dare say.' Her heart began to beat a little faster at the thought. 'But not yet. That would appear very rude to Georgina and Andrew, wouldn't it?'

'Yes,' he agreed ruefully, 'I suppose it would. So we stay on the floor.'

'We stay on the floor,' she agreed. 'At least the music is good. Dave and Pete are excellent DJs. Do you like Simply Red?' she added after a moment.

'Simply what?' he asked.

She stepped back and looked up into his face. 'The group,' she said, wondering yet again if he was winding her up. 'Don't tell me you haven't heard of them because I won't believe you.'

'Well, I'm sorry but you're just going to have to disbelieve me.'

'You mean. . .?' she stared at him.

'I've never heard of them in my life.'

Because they had been so preoccupied when they had first taken to the dance floor, Kate had remained unaware of his closeness. Now, as she laughed when she realised he was telling the truth about never having heard of the pop group and as he tightened his grip, drawing her even closer, she could no longer—even subconsciously—deny the intimacy of the moment.

Although Jon might well have never heard of Simply Red, she thought as he held her close, the sensuality of the music and poignancy of the lyrics seemed to possess him and in turn transmit themselves to her.

It was a long time since she'd been held by a man in this way, she realised with a little shock, and never had she been held by a man like Jon Hammond. A man with so much vitality, so much unleashed power in that deceptively lithe frame. She could feel it now, the sinews in his arms and the muscles rippling across his shoulders.

This was a man who'd led a tough life, a hard life, and

who'd learned to fend for himself. A man not to be trifled with, who could give as good as he got. She gave a little shiver at the thought, but as his cheek brushed hers she sensed a tenderness in him and recognised his gentleness and the yearning to be loved.

After all, hadn't she too craved love once. . .?

She stirred restlessly in his arms and he stared down at her. 'Penny for them,' he said.

'For what?'

'Your thoughts. You were miles away,' he said softly against the silky chestnut sheen of her dark hair.

'Was I?' she protested. 'Well, maybe I was. But I doubt they were worth even a penny.'

'Is that a fact?' he breathed. Holding her away from him, he looked down into her eyes. If that's the case, maybe it's time they were forgotten for good.'

'Yes,' she agreed, 'maybe it is.'

They danced for most of the evening, returning only briefly to their table for refreshment and Patsy Hogan's non-stop chatter before escaping again.

'I dare say we could make our excuses now,' Kate murmured at last when exhaustion threatened to get the better of them both.

'That's fine for you,' Jon replied with a laugh, 'but really, you know, I have to wait for Helen.'

'Oh?'

'She gave me a lift here,' he replied.

'Oh,' said Kate, 'I see.'

They danced on in silence for a moment, then he said, 'Unless of course. . .'

'Yes? Unless what?'

'I could persuade you to run me home. . .?'

'Why not?' She heard herself answer quite plainly.

It was, after all, a reasonable request, so why was it that deep inside she felt a sudden, sharp thrill at the thought of being alone with him again?

CHAPTER NINE

'THEY'RE going to Venice for a second honeymoon,' said
Kate as she and Jon drove away from the Shalbrooke.

'Is that where they spent their first?'

'Apparently so.' Kate nodded. 'Very romantic—all
those bridges and gondolas.'

'I think I'll settle for starlit African skies, and sunsets
you wouldn't believe.' He gave a low, contented chuckle,
then added, 'You know something, Kate? I've enjoyed
tonight.'

'So have I,' she agreed, and realised she meant it. 'I
haven't danced so much for years—and that's all thanks
to Patsy Hogan.'

She drove on through Porchfield into Carisbrooke and
on to Gatcombe, happy and comfortable in Jon's company. As she turned into the drive they could both see
lights in the Coach House. Bringing the car to a halt on
the gravel drive in front of the stable block, neither of
them made any attempt to get out and Kate rested her
arms on the steering-wheel.

'What's happening with Harry tonight?' she asked,
staring across at the lighted windows.

'Helen arranged a sitter for him,' Jon said. 'I doubt
he's been very happy. In fact,' he added, 'I would say
he's become quite aggressive in the last few days.'

'I'll come over and see him again in a day or so,' said
Kate. She paused. 'I feel so sorry for Helen. She has very
little life of her own at the moment. Take tonight, for

instance—there'll be no going on anywhere with Richard because she'll have to get back here to release the sitter.'

'Talking of going on somewhere,' said Jon, 'you will come in and have coffee with me, won't you?'

He was climbing out of the car as he spoke and Kate hesitated for only a moment. She was as certain as she could be that Jon Hammond was all right and that she had nothing to fear. She felt she'd got to know him fairly well since he'd arrived, and she had to admit she had thoroughly enjoyed the evening they had just spent in each other's company. She got out of the car and followed him towards the old stable block.

'Hold on a minute,' he said. 'I'll put a light on. Don't want you falling on these stairs.'

She waited in the darkness as Jon fumbled for the light switch. Seconds later light flooded the yard and he ran ahead of her up the staircase and unlocked the door of the stable flat. Kate followed more slowly and by the time she reached the top he was waiting for her in the tiny kitchen.

She paused in the doorway and looked round at the stripped pine cupboards and dark blue ceramic tiles. 'We used to play up here,' she said slowly. 'I used to stay with Helen sometimes for the weekend if I didn't go home from school. The last time I came in here it was very much just a room over the stables—lots of cobwebs, straw and tack. . .'

'I must say it's a very comfortable flat now,' said Jon, taking the kettle to the sink and filling it. 'I've only instant coffee, I'm afraid. None of that fancy filter stuff you use.'

'Instant's fine,' said Kate. She was still gazing around, trying to adapt to the change. 'I can hardly believe this is the same place,' she said as she watched Jon take two mugs and a jar of coffee from a cupboard.

'Have a look at the rest of it,' he said, taking a carton of milk out of the fridge. 'It won't take you long.'

He was right. It didn't take long. In the time it took for the kettle to come to the boil Kate had seen all there was to see—the sitting room through an archway directly off the kitchen, with its pine dresser and chintz-covered sofa, the main bedroom with its *en suite* shower room and cream quilted bedcovers and one smaller room, complete with bunk beds.

'Helen usually lets this throughout the entire season,' said Kate as she wandered back and joined him in the kitchen. 'It's only been this year, because of Harry, that it's not been let to visitors.'

'I can only stay for three months,' he said. 'Just until Helen's cousin arrives. But at least I shall have time to look around for somewhere else.'

It was on the tip of her tongue to ask him when he planned to return to Africa. But something stopped her. Quite suddenly, she simply didn't want to know. He was here, and for the time being she was happy for it to remain that way.

He carried the two mugs through to the sitting room, and as Kate followed him and sat down on the sofa her eye fell on a table lamp on a small desk beneath the window. There was something familiar about the lamp, but just for the moment she couldn't think what it was. Jon put the coffee onto a low table, before easing his long frame down onto the sofa beside her.

They talked easily as they sipped their coffee—of Kate's childhood when she and Helen and Diana had played together, of Jon's work in Africa, of practice business and of the evening they had both enjoyed.

'I haven't danced like that for a very long time,' said Kate with a little sigh.

'Took me back to my student days,' said Jon.

Kate laughed. 'Yes, it does take you back. It took me back to. . .to. . .' She trailed off. She had been about to say that the dancing and the music had taken her back to the parties she had attended while she had been working at Barts, but that might have led to talking of Alistair—and the last thing she wanted was to talk about Alistair.

In fact, the last thing she wanted was to even think about Alistair. . .especially now. . .when she was here with Jon. . .

Turning abruptly, she put her mug on a cabinet beside the sofa, and as she did so her eye caught the lamp again. In that instant she remembered what it was the lamp reminded her of. It was a pretty lamp, its pale green shade fringed with long crystal beads. They had had one in the flat she and Alistair had shared, only theirs had been blue and not green.

Jon was talking again. Abruptly she turned back to him. They talked on, getting to know each other's tastes, and almost consciously Kate felt herself relax. It was warm and comfortable here in this cosy flat beside this man who, in such a short space of time, she had come to think of as her friend. Even when she realised that his arm was resting lightly along the back of the sofa behind her she felt safe, not threatened in any way. And when at last he moved closer to her she was quite happy to rest her head on his shoulder.

'Kate,' he said after a while, 'can we do this again some time? Go out together, I mean? Maybe a meal? I can't remember an evening when I've enjoyed myself so much. . .'

'Me neither,' she said. 'Yes, Jon, I'd like that.'

She lifted her face in anticipation as his hand moved to her jaw, his fingers becoming entangled in her hair.

His lips felt warm and gentle against her own. She stiffened, but only slightly, as she felt his tongue part her lips, then she relaxed again, closing her eyes as he drew her fully into his arms.

It was a very long time since she'd been kissed like this. His body felt hard against the softness of her own. She sensed his growing arousal and recognised the leap of desire deep inside herself, something she had doubted she would ever feel again.

His kiss grew deeper, more demanding. Then Kate realised that very gradually he was easing her further back onto the sofa and she felt the first flutter of alarm deep inside her, like that of a butterfly that is trapped.

Her eyes snapped open. Immediately she caught sight of the green beaded lamp, and a wave of panic swept over her, threatening to engulf her.

She began to struggle, but to Jon her struggles must have been totally ineffectual. His body was almost covering her own. He was big, and he was strong. She could feel the strength of the muscles in his arms.

Terror filled her throat, almost choking her, as with one last, final effort she summoned enough strength to push him away.

'Kate. . .!' He was staring at her in bewilderment.

Sobbing and gasping, she scrambled to her feet.

'Kate,' he said again. 'Whatever is it? What's wrong?'

'I'm sorry.' She took a couple of deep, searing breaths as she struggled to regain control. 'I'm sorry. I just can't. . .that's all.'

'But what did you think I was going to do, for God's

sake?' He stared at her in shocked silence.

'Nothing, Jon. Nothing. Like I said, I'm sorry. It's me, it's not you. I shouldn't have come back here with you. It's my fault.'

'I don't get it.' He shook his head. 'Why shouldn't you have come back? It seemed the most natural thing in the world to me.' He still looked bewildered. 'We had a pleasant evening—'

'I'm sorry, Jon,' Kate said again. 'It's like I said. It isn't your fault. I'd better go. . .' Blindly she groped her way across the room.

'Kate, you can't go like this. I can't let you drive yourself home—'

'I'm perfectly all right. Really I am. Please, Jon, just leave me alone.'

He followed her down the stairs and stood in the doorway as she got into her car. She was still shaking as she started the engine and, with barely a backward glance, drove away. She passed a car about a hundred yards further on in the lane, but in her haste barely noticed it.

'Was that Kate?' Helen climbed out of her car and peered through the darkness towards the figure silhouetted against the lights of the stable block.

'Yes.' Jon replied abruptly.

'I thought it was. She seemed in a bit of a hurry.' Helen paused. 'Is everything all right?'

'You tell me.' He shook his head. 'I'm sure I don't know.'

Helen stared at him but in the darkness was unable to distinguish his features, let alone read his expression. His tone of voice, however, indicated that all wasn't quite right. 'I thought you and Kate seemed to be enjoying yourselves at the party,' she said.

'So did I,' he replied tightly. 'Just shows how wrong you can be, doesn't it?'

'What do you mean?' asked Helen in growing dismay. All evening she'd been hoping that she was reading the signs correctly and that something seemed to be happening between Kate and Jon.

'No one warned me I was dealing with the original ice maiden,' he said with a short, bitter laugh.

'Kate?' Helen blinked. 'Are you sure we're talking about the same person?'

'Well, I don't see anyone else around.' He turned to go back up the stairs.

'Jon,' she said quickly, 'don't go. Listen, let me release Gwen, my sitter, so that she can go home and then come over for a chat.'

'What for?'

'Well, you're obviously upset. . .and, I must admit, I'm a bit concerned about Kate. She must have seen me in the lane, must have known it was me. But she drove by like a bat out of hell. . . Didn't wave or flash her lights or anything to even acknowledge that she'd seen me.'

Jon didn't answer.

'Please, Jon,' she said. 'I'm really concerned.'

'OK,' he said at last. 'I'll just go upstairs and shut the door.'

Ten minutes later, after Helen had watched Gwen drive away and checked that her father was sleeping peacefully, she let Jon into the house. In the kitchen she offered him tea or coffee.

He shook his head. 'No, thanks,' he said wryly. 'We actually had coffee, believe it or not.'

'So, what went wrong, for heaven's sake?' Helen stared at him as he slumped into a chair at the kitchen table and covered his face with his hands.

'God knows.' He lowered his hands. 'We seemed to be getting on really well. We had a great evening, Helen, we really did.' He looked up at her, his expression helpless. 'We talked. We danced. . .in fact, we danced all the evening. . . At first it was so we wouldn't have to put up with Patsy's chatter. . . Sorry, Helen, but that's the way it was. . .'

'Don't apologise.' Helen pulled a face. 'She's the bane of Richard's life.'

'Later,' Jon continued, 'I could have sworn we were dancing because we wanted to. Then afterwards, when we came back here, I invited her in for coffee. She seemed quite happy with that. We talked some more. . .about our jobs. . .about all sorts of things, everything really. . . She seemed so relaxed, so happy, but then. . .' He stopped.

'Yes,' Helen prompted. 'Then?'

He looked a little embarrassed but he took a deep breath and went on, 'When I attempted to take things a stage further her reaction was. . .' He spread his hands, and when Helen continued to stare at him in silence, he added, 'I only tried to kiss her for God's sake, Helen. She fought me off like a wildcat.'

Helen remained silent for a moment, then she said slowly, 'You know, Jon, this is so unlike Kate. It's almost as if you're talking about someone else, just like it was when you were telling me about her being so nervous. It didn't sound like Kate then, and it certainly doesn't now.'

'What are you saying?'

'I'm thinking that your theory may be right.' She paused, and when Jon looked at her questioningly she went on, 'You said before you thought Kate had been badly frightened at some stage. At the time I practically dismissed the idea. It just seemed so improbable somehow, even your idea of Kate being nervous. But now, in view of her reactions this evening, I think you could be right.'

'What do you think we should do about it?' asked Jon. 'I don't want to frighten her off even more.'

'You've become fond of her, haven't you, Jon?' asked Helen quietly.

'Yes, Helen, I have.' He nodded. 'I haven't felt this way about a woman for a very long time, but I recognise the fact that she has a problem and I know I need to tread very carefully.'

'Will you let me see what I can do?' asked Helen. 'I'll try and talk to her and in a roundabout way find out what this is all about.'

'What do you think I should do?'

'Just act naturally,' Helen replied firmly. 'Carry on as if this incident tonight hadn't happened.'

He remained silent, staring down at his hands which he had tightened into fists. At last, unclenching them, he stood up and looked at Helen.

'All right,' he said. 'See what you can do.'

Kate wasn't sure how she got through the rest of that Easter weekend. She was dreading having to face Jon in surgery on Tuesday morning. She couldn't imagine what he must have thought of her and of the way she had behaved towards him. The panic attacks she had experienced ever since the break-up with Alistair had grown fewer but, as Saturday night had proved, obviously hadn't disappeared altogether.

She'd so enjoyed the evening in Jon's company and everything had been fine until he'd tried to take things further. Somehow she had seemed totally unable to cope with the prospect of what might follow. Then the sight of that wretched lamp seemed to have triggered unwanted memories and brought on another of the dreaded attacks.

Maybe, she told her herself as the weekend ground slowly on, maybe she should just try explaining everything to Jon. He was a doctor, after all—he should understand.

But somehow even the thought of telling him, of telling anyone for that matter, what had happened made her shudder with horror. She still doubted whether anyone would believe her, and even if they did she would then have to contend with the embarrassment of them knowing.

By the time Tuesday morning arrived Kate had worked herself up to such a state that when she finally saw Jon she was amazed when he appeared perfectly natural and made no reference whatsoever to what had happened.

Surgery was brisk, as it usually was, following a bank holiday. Kate had almost completed her list when she glanced at the remaining name and saw to her surprise that it was Pete Steel who was her last patient. The paramedic had been one of the patients Kate had inherited from Richard Fleetwood's father when he had retired, but she couldn't remember ever seeing him in surgery before.

'Hello, Pete,' she said, as he pushed open the door and looked warily into the room.

'Morning, Dr Chapman.' He nodded and came right inside.

'It's not often we see you here,' Kate said, then added, 'Come in and sit down.' She watched as he took the seat opposite her desk. 'You and Dave did very well on

Saturday night.' She said it to try to relax him because she couldn't help but notice that he seemed tense and ill at ease.

'We try,' he said abruptly.

Kate got the impression that he didn't want to talk about the disco and that he needed to get on with what he had come to say—needed in some way to get it over with.

'So,' she said, glancing down at his record envelope which appeared very sparse, 'what seems to be the problem?'

'I'm not really sure,' he replied hesitantly. 'I know there's something wrong but I can't really put my finger on what it is.'

'What symptoms have you been having?'

'Well, I can only really describe them as a form of clumsiness,' said Pete. 'A sort of lack of co-ordination. At first I didn't take too much notice of it. It seemed to start with a tingling feeling in my right hand, and at other times the hand and arm felt numb. It always went away and I tried not to worry about it but. . .'

'Yes?' Kate looked up when he stopped. 'But what?'

Pete averted his gaze. 'This time my wife's noticed. She said I've slowed down recently—that I always seem to be tired.'

'Do you feel tired, Pete?' asked Kate.

He nodded. 'Yes, if I'm honest, I do. I used to play football, but I don't seem to have the energy for that these days. Even playing with the kids seems to wear me out.'

'Let's see, how old are you?' Kate glanced at the computer screen where she had just called up Pete Steel's details. 'Ah, thirty-three, is that right?'

He nodded. 'Yes, although I have to say there have been times just recently when I've felt more like sixty-three.'

'How about the job? Have you been coping there all right?'

'Reasonably, but I must admit I've been getting concerned with this numbness. I've had a few nightmares about dropping a patient. Both my wife and Dave—you know, Dave Morey—have commented that they've thought there's something wrong.'

'Are you eating well, Pete?' asked Kate. When he nodded she added, 'And sleeping?'

'Yes. Like I said, I'm so tired all the time.'

'Not depressed or worried about anything?'

'Not particularly.' He shrugged. 'Just the usual worries, of course, about paying the mortgage and things like that, but nothing out of the ordinary.'

'Any pain anywhere?'

'No, only the tingling and the numbness.'

'Right, then, Pete.' Kate stood up. 'I'd like to check your blood pressure and I'll arrange for you to come back for a blood test.'

Five minutes later, as Pete prepared to leave the room, he paused at the door and looked back at Kate.

'You don't think it's anything too awful, do you, Dr Chapman?'

'It's far too soon to say what it might be, Pete,' Kate replied briskly. Catching sight of the scared expression that flitted across his features, she added more gently, 'Try not to worry—I'm sure it isn't anything we can't put right.'

Thoughtfully she watched as he left the room. She hoped the numbness wasn't the start of something debilitating. She liked Pete Steel. He and Dave Morey made a cheerful team. But while Dave Morey had a reputation for being a bit of a lad Pete, in contrast, was a family man—a loving husband and father.

As Pete was her last patient of the morning she made her way out to Reception. There seemed to be some good-natured bantering going on behind the reception desk between Jon and Martin Hogan.

Carefully Kate avoided Jon's gaze and spoke to Claire. 'Do I have many house calls, Claire?'

Claire checked her book. 'Four, Dr Chapman,' she replied. 'The last one has just come in. Helen Turner phoned to ask if you could call in to see her father when you've finished today.'

Kate looked up sharply, her gaze briefly meeting Jon's. 'Did she say what the problem was?'

'Only that he was very aggressive this morning and she felt she needed to talk to you,' Claire replied.

'I'll go over later.' She picked up the records, but as she turned to leave Reception Jon fell into step beside her.

'Helen's quite right,' he said. 'Harry was very aggressive this morning.'

'You saw him?' She threw him a quick glance.

'Yes. Helen called out to me.'

'She should have called me in,' said Kate, suddenly on the defensive. 'Harry is my patient. I told Helen she could call me at any time of the day or night.'

'It wasn't like that,' said Jon. 'I just happened to be there—on the premises, that's all. Helen needed physical help in restraining Harry—not necessarily medical help, although I guess that has to follow now.'

'Quite,' she said tightly. After a moment's silence she said, 'So what happened?'

'Apparently, Harry came downstairs into the kitchen. He wanted to make tea which, according to Helen, he frequently does. For some reason this morning something went wrong. He wasn't able to do what he wanted and he became very frustrated. He threw the kettle of boiling water across the kitchen.'

'Good God.' Kate threw him a startled glance. 'Was Helen hurt?'

'No she managed to get out of the way, luckily. But afterwards he was very agitated and had to be restrained. I managed to calm him down. Helen eventually got his medication into him and after a while he was as quiet as a lamb.'

'Until the next time,' said Kate, biting her lip.

'Yes,' agreed Jon. 'Until the next time.'

'I'll go over there,' said Kate.

They walked in silence down the corridor. As they reached her room she stopped with one hand on the handle and said awkwardly, 'About Saturday, Jon. . .'

'It's OK,' he said quickly.

'No,' she said, 'it isn't OK. I'm sorry, Jon. I really am. I don't know what came over me. . .but I just wanted you to know that it wasn't anything to do with you.'

'It's all right, Kate,' he said softly. 'It really is. But, you know, it's like I said to you before—it sometimes helps to talk about these things.'

'Yes,' she said quickly and looked away unable to meet his gaze. 'Yes, I know. But I'm not sure I can.'

'Well, don't forget, I'm a good listener.'

'I won't, and. . .thanks, Jon, for being so understanding.'

He walked away down the corridor to his own room and she watched him for a moment before going into her consulting room. Inside she leaned against the door and briefly closed her eyes. If only she could bring herself to tell him. If only she could find the words that would unleash that dreadful panic which seemed trapped for ever inside her. In her heart she knew she should tell someone.

If only it was that easy.

He had said she could talk to him. That he would listen. He had seemed interested in her, as if he had wanted to take their friendship further. She, in turn, was deeply attracted to him. She knew that now, just as she had recognised those first stirrings of desire inside herself and had sensed the passion behind his kiss.

She had ruined it all, of course, by clamming up the way she had and then, if that hadn't been enough, by bolting out of the flat like a startled rabbit. He must have thought her a silly, neurotic woman. She doubted if he would want to try again. No man would after being treated like that. And if he did would she be any different? Would the day ever come when those demons would no longer be there?

Fighting sudden tears that sprang to her eyes, she took her jacket from the hook on the door. Work was the only antidote to her problem, just as it had been for the last five years. Angrily brushing the tears away, she struggled into her jacket, grabbed her case and car keys and hurried from the room.

CHAPTER TEN

'I REALLY think the time has come, Helen,' said Kate.

'I know.' Helen gave a deep sigh. 'I know it has, just as I know that you are absolutely right, but. . . Oh, I don't know. It's just that I had kidded myself I would be able to cope. . .would be able to let him stay at home with me until the end. I know that is what he would have wanted.'

'That may be so,' said Kate, 'but for the time being I think we only need to be talking about respite care, say, for just part of each week.'

'He'll hate it,' said Helen. 'He simply won't understand.'

'But if he could understand,' said Kate, 'Harry would be the first to agree that you needed a break. Honestly, Helen, you can't keep this up for much longer, you know. All these sleepless nights, the round-the-clock care, the demands of your job—your own health will start to deteriorate soon if you aren't very careful.'

'That's what Richard says,' said Helen ruefully.

'Well, there you are, then.' Kate paused. 'And talking of Richard—it can't be too easy on him either, can it, relationship-wise, with you being so tied to the house?'

'I know.' Helen sighed. 'I'm lucky, I suppose, where Richard is concerned. I guess a lot of men wouldn't have put up with the situation but, well, Richard is different. He understands, what with being a doctor and having nursed Diana through her illness.'

'Even so, you can't expect him to wait for ever. Let's

148

face it, Helen,' Kate said with a smile, 'none of us is getting any younger.'

'Don't remind me.' Helen pulled a face. 'But while we're on that subject how about you?'

'How about me?' asked Kate lightly. The two of them were sitting on the seat outside the back door in the afternoon sunshine, and she turned her head slightly to throw a sidelong glance at her friend.

'Well, there doesn't seem to have been a lot happening on the romantic front for you in the last few years.'

Kate shrugged. 'I'm different,' she said. 'I gave up on the marriage stakes some time ago but you. . .well, you always wanted to settle down, to have children. . .'

Helen frowned. 'I didn't know you'd given up on the marriage stakes.'

'Well, I have. I decided it just wasn't worth all the hassle. I came to the conclusion that my career was more satisfying than any man.'

Helen was silent for a moment then she said quietly, 'Does this have anything to do with Alistair?'

'It might do.' Kate shrugged, wishing she could change the subject. She was still feeling raw from recent events, without reopening any old wounds.

'I never did understand what went wrong between you two,' said Helen slowly. 'I know I only met him twice, but he seemed a really nice guy and the two of you seemed well suited.' She hesitated, then glanced at Kate again. 'So, what did go wrong, Kate?'

'It just didn't work out, that's all,' Kate replied quickly. 'We weren't as well suited as I thought. I guess it was a good job we were only living together and that we hadn't actually tied the knot.'

'Have you seen him since?' asked Helen after a

moment. 'It must be, what, four years or so since you came back here?'

'Five, actually,' replied Kate. 'And, no, I haven't seen him since.' She was silent for a long moment, apparently studying the polyanthus in Helen's flower border. Coming to a sudden decision, she said, 'He went to America to work.'

'Really?' Helen sounded surprised. 'You never said.'

'There didn't seem any point in mentioning it. The affair was over by then. But about two years ago. . .' Kate swallowed and hesitated, but before she could change her mind she rushed on. 'I had a letter from his sister to say. . .to say he had been killed in a road accident.' She continued to study the flowers in the border, but this time without really seeing them. Turning her head at last, she found that Helen was staring at her in shocked silence.

'It's OK,' she said quickly. 'Don't worry. I'm over it.'

'But, Kate,' Helen sounded aghast, 'Why ever didn't you say? Why didn't you tell me? I had no idea.'

'There didn't really seem much point in telling anyone,' said Kate slowly. 'The relationship was over. It had ended three years before. . .before Alistair's death. I just didn't feel I could talk about it to anyone. . .not even to you, Helen,' she added defensively.

'Oh, Kate.' Helen still looked stricken. 'I'm so sorry. Really I am. But I do wish I'd known. I wish you could have told me.'

'What good would it have done?'

'I don't know,' said Helen helplessly. 'Simply that I would like to have been there for you, I guess.' They were silent for a while after that, each busy with her own thoughts. In the end it was Helen who broke the silence. 'Has there been no one since?' she asked at last.

'Not really.' Kate blinked and shook her head.

'But that doesn't mean to say there won't be,' said Helen passionately.

'I'm not that bothered,' Kate began, trying desperately to put sudden, disturbing images of Jon Hammond out of her mind.

Then, almost as if she could read her thoughts, Helen spoke again. 'I thought you seemed to be getting on rather well with Jon the other night,' she said.

'What do you mean?' Kate tried to keep her tone light, casual, knowing full well what Helen meant but at the same time playing for time—seeking the right answers, answers that wouldn't give rise to further speculation on her friend's part.

'At the party,' Helen persisted. 'Every time I looked up the pair of you seemed to be dancing together.'

'That was the only way to get away from Patsy Hogan.' Kate attempted a flippant laugh.

'It didn't look as if it was only that. Not from where I was sitting,' said Helen crisply. 'And he is rather nice. You have to admit that, Kate.'

'Yes, I suppose he is,' Kate agreed at last.

'He's caused quite a stir amongst my staff, I can tell you,' Helen went on.

'That doesn't surprise me. Our receptionists are pretty smitten, too,' admitted Kate wryly.

'Well, he is unusual, you have to admit. A far cry from the average locum or houseman we get round here. The gossip around my girls, though. . .' Helen shot her a sly glance '. . .is that there's not a lot of point in pursuing him.'

'You mean because he isn't here for long?' asked Kate.

'No,' Helen shook her head. 'No, that isn't the reason.

It's because everyone says he's besotted with you. That he can't take his eyes off you.'

'What! Oh, for goodness' sake,' Kate protested, but at Helen's words her heart had begun to beater faster.

'Is that so improbable?' asked Helen, raising her eyebrows.

'I don't know about improbable.' Kate gave a short laugh. 'More like ridiculous.' She stood up as she spoke and Helen looked up at her, shielding her eyes from the sun. 'I don't see why,' she said. 'Don't you like him?'

'Of course I like him,' said Kate. 'You can't really not like him, can you?'

'Well, then,' said Helen, 'Why not just enjoy it?'

'I can't see a lot of point in getting involved,' said Kate.

'Why not?' Helen got to her feet.

'He'll go back to Africa,' said Kate, 'and where would that leave me?'

'Why not just live for the moment and enjoy it while it lasts?' said Helen softly. When Kate didn't answer they turned to go back into the house.

She left a little later, after telling Helen that she would be making arrangements immediately for the respite care for Harry which was so urgently needed.

Live for the moment. Enjoy it while it lasts, Helen had said, thought Kate as she drove home. If only it was that simple. Really, she would like nothing better than to enjoy a brief, passionate fling with Jon Hammond because that was probably all it would be, given the short time he was to be with them, but somehow she doubted whether she was capable of such a thing.

Maybe she would have been once, before Alistair, but not now. He had changed all that. She was amazed she'd actually told Helen about Alistair's death. She hadn't told anyone else—had tried to blot it right out of her mind, along with those other things that were too disturbing to think about.

When she had received the letter from his sister, telling her what had happened, she had felt desperately shocked. But then the anger had set in. Anger that the whole business would now remain unresolved, and that Alistair's death had somehow prevented him from being called to task for what he had done. Not that she could ever have been the one to have him called to task. She had just wanted him out of her life for ever, wanted as much distance between them as possible. Which was why she had felt so relieved when she had heard he'd gone to the States to work.

Why his death had come as such a shock—had thown her equilibrium so much—she was still at a loss to explain, even after all this time.

She had to put him in the past where he belonged, she knew that. She had to let her life move on, maybe form new relationships, even find love again. She had pretended to Helen that none of that mattered, that she wasn't interested. But that wasn't the truth. Really, she would like nothing better than to settle down with the right man and perhaps have children.

Helen had suggested that Jon Hammond was interested in her. Kate's pulse raced again at the thought. Not that Jon was the marrying kind, of course. But it was true he had seemed interested—until that dreadful moment when she had behaved like an hysterical teenager. She doubted whether he was interested now. Not after that.

But how could she overcome this fear, this panic, this legacy from Alistair? How could she ever learn to relax and to trust a man again?

*   *   *

After Kate had driven away Helen went slowly back into the house. They had left her father in his bedroom but he had got up and was now in the kitchen. He was muttering angrily to himself and banging mugs and plates on the tiled work surface.

'Don't do that, Dad,' said Helen wearily. 'You'll break them.'

'What do you know?' He swung round on her sharply. For a moment his eyes blazed wildly, and he lifted a mug as if he was about to throw it across the kitchen.

'Let me have that.' Fearing another scene similar to the one earlier that day where she had been forced to call Jon for help, Helen held out her hand for the mug. Defiantly Harry glared back at her, for all the world like a naughty child in the middle of a tantrum. Steadily she stared back, maintaining eye contact with him.

'What do you know?' he said again, but this time he mumbled it and there was less aggression in his tone.

'Come on, Dad,' she said, gently now.

'What do you know?' he whispered, and with a look almost of despair that tore at her heart he meekly handed her the mug, then sat down in the rocking chair beside the Aga.

'We'll make some tea,' she said. As she was filling the kettle a car came up the drive and she glanced out of the kitchen window. 'Here comes Jon,' she said. 'Perhaps he'd like a cup as well.'

'What do you know?' said Harry vacantly.

Helen opened the window, and as Jon got out of his car she called out to him. 'We were just about to make some tea, Jon. Would you care to join us?'

'Thanks. I'd love to,' he called back.

Helen spooned tea into the teapot. Jon pushed open the

back door and, ducking under the low beam, came into the kitchen. Harry didn't even look up, instead rocking backwards and forwards and repeating to himself over and over again the phrase which now seemed entrenched in his brain.

'Hello, Harry,' said Jon as he sat down at the table.

'What do you know?' mumbled Harry. 'What do you know?'

Jon glanced questioningly at Helen, who shook her head. 'Kate's been in,' she said. 'You've only just missed her.'

'I didn't see her on the road,' he said quickly.

'Maybe she went the other way.'

'Yes, maybe,' he replied.

'What do you know?' said Harry.

'Did she come to see Harry?' asked Jon.

Helen nodded. 'Yes, I asked her to come in. I need some help, Jon.' She sighed as she brewed the tea.

'Well, I'm glad you've recognised the fact,' he said quietly.

'I feel guilty when he's like this,' she said after a moment, throwing her father a tender glance, 'but when he gets aggressive I just can't handle him. Kate's gone back to the surgery to arrange some respite care for us.'

'It's not before time, Helen,' said Jon. 'You've done a marvellous job with Harry and you mustn't feel guilty, you know.' He turned his head as Harry suddenly struggled to his feet and, still muttering to himself, shuffled out of the room.

Helen sat heavily down at the table with the teapot and cups in front of her. For several moments she was silent, her eyes bright with unshed tears as she reflected on the events of the last hour. At last, with another sigh, she appeared to pull herself together.

'Kate and I talked, Jon,' she said as she poured the tea.

He looked up quickly. 'You mean. . .?'

She nodded and handed him his cup. 'Yes, and we were wrong, you know, quite wrong.'

'Really?' he stared at her. 'In what way?'

'In thinking that she had been frightened. That that was the reason for her apparent nervousness. It isn't that at all, you know.'

'You mean she talked? She told you?'

Helen nodded. 'Maybe I'm sticking my neck out here by telling you because I gather, from what she said, she hasn't told anyone else. She didn't, however, say it was in confidence, and because I know that you care about her. . .'

'I more than care about her,' he said softly.

'Yes, well, that's what I thought,' said Helen.

'Is it anything to do with the guy she was living with, the one you mentioned?'

'Alistair Cunningham?' Helen paused. 'Yes, I would say it has everything to do with him. But not in quite the way we thought. I don't think it is anything to do with why they split up—it is more to do with what happened afterwards,' she added slowly.

'How do you mean—afterwards?' Jon stared at her across the table.

'Well, apparently, Alistair Cunningham went to the States to work and a couple of years ago Kate heard that he had been killed in a road accident.'

'Good grief!' Jon looked astonished. 'And she never said anything?'

Helen shook her head. 'I've been wondering, in view

of what you said, whether she's been suffering from some sort of delayed shock or whether maybe she even blames herself in some way.'

'Why should she do that?'

'Well, maybe she was the one to end the relationship, causing him to go abroad.'

'That would hardly make it her fault—what happened to him afterwards.'

'That's true,' Helen agreed. 'But the mind can play funny tricks and maybe if she hasn't been able to come to terms with his death, hasn't been able to grieve for him, she could in some way be blaming herself. What do you think?' Thoughtfully she stirred her tea.

'Well, it's certainly a possibility,' said Jon slowly. 'And if that is the case I suppose it could account for her rather strange behaviour.' He paused, sipped his tea and said reflectively, 'So, if it is that, where would you say that leaves me?'

Picking up her cup, Helen stared at him over the rim. 'Oh, I would say you could well be in with a chance,' she said. 'But, having said that, I would also say you would have to proceed with caution. Take things very slowly. Don't rush her in any way.'

'Did she mention me?' There was no disguising the eagerness in his voice now and Helen smiled.

'She might have done,' she said.

'But you're not going to tell me what she said—is that it?' He raised one eyebrow.

'There are some things that are absolutely sacrosanct,' said Helen firmly, 'and girl talk is one of them. I've told you enough. The rest is up to you.'

CHAPTER ELEVEN

SUNLIGHT sparkled on the water and at first the coloured speck was little more than a smudge on the horizon, but as Kate stopped the car and wound down her window she knew it was *Mistral*'s gold and blue spinnaker she could see in the Solent.

Jon Hammond was on board at Richard Fleetwood's invitation, and Kate could hardly wait to see whether or not he had enjoyed the experience. In fact, she thought with a little sigh as she stepped out of the car and stood, shielding her eyes from the sun and watching as the yacht crept closer, these days Jon Hammond seemed to fill most of her thoughts.

It had happened subtly, almost without her realising it. As spring had nudged its way into early summer somehow, quietly, Jon seemed always to be there. Not just at work, which would have been understandable—inevitable, even—but on other occasions. Socially—at a dinner party given by Andrew and Georgina Merrick with Helen and Richard making up a sixsome, at a barbeque a couple of weeks later at Richard Fleetwood's house at Newtown Creek and then at a drinks party at the Hogans'. And casually, appearing at the most unexpected moments—as she shopped in the supermarket, once while she was exercising Helen's dog, Chester, in the woods around Gatcombe and another time while she was swimming in the local pool and he just happened to be there at the same time.

At one time all this might have irritated Kate, but as time went on she grew used to his presence and came to enjoy and to expect it—to such an extent that she felt real disappointment on the occasions when he didn't appear.

The embarrassment of that evening in the stable flat appeared to have been forgotten, much to Kate's relief, for he had never once referred to it. But while it seemed not to have altered his attitude towards her neither had he attempted the same level of intimacy again.

And Kate wasn't certain how she felt about that.

On the one hand she was relieved, not wanting to have to cope with another possible panic attack, but on the other she had found herself anticipating some advance from him and being desperately disappointed when it hadn't happened.

On one occasion, after the barbeque, he had taken her home, and when she had invited him in to her apartment—and he had declined—they had sat together in his car and watched a particularly spectacular sunset. It had been at that moment that she had ached for him to touch her—to take her into his arms, to feel his lips on hers the way she had before—only this time without the panic which had followed.

Instead, he had merely touched her cheek and murmured goodnight, leaving her no alternative other than to get out of the car and watch in frustration as he drove away.

Maybe he wasn't interested in her in that way any more, she thought now as she watched *Mistral* sail into harbour. Maybe he thought her cold and unloving.

If only he knew. Turning, she climbed back into her car and started the engine. If she hurried she could drive round to the marina as they moored. Be there as they arrived.

She was only just in time, parking the car and walking down the wooden slats of the marina as they tied up alongside.

'Hello, there,' she called, and as Jon looked up her heart gave a sudden lurch because there could be no mistaking the look of pure pleasure on his face as he caught sight of her. In borrowed sailing gear and deck shoes and with his fair hair ruffled from the sea breeze, he looked happy and relaxed. There had been no recurrence of the virus which had brought him back from Africa and he seemed to have fully recovered his strength.

'How did it go?' Briefly Kate's gaze flickered to Richard who smiled at her and nodded. 'He's a natural,' he said. 'Some people just are.'

'I've agreed to take Richard on safari in return,' said Jon with a grin.

At the mention of safaris and Jon's eventual return to Tanzania Kate's heart sank. She simply couldn't imagine life now without him.

The two men joined her a little later, and they walked the short distance to the yacht club where they stopped in the bar for a drink.

Kate was on call and just as they had almost finished their drinks her pager went off. After taking the call on the club's telephone, she returned to the bar.

'I shall have to go,' she said. 'One of my patients has been discharged from hospital post-operative and is requiring analgesics.'

'Will you be going back to the centre?' asked Jon.

'Afterwards, yes,' Kate replied.

'Can I come with you?' He drained his glass. 'My car

is at the centre. It'll save Richard taking me back there. He's meeting Helen for lunch.'

'Sure.' Kate nodded, secretly pleased that the time with Jon was not about to be cut short.

'I'm glad you enjoyed your first taste of sailing,' she said a few minutes later as they headed for the patient's home in the nearby village of Gurnard.

'It was wonderful,' he agreed. 'Much more exciting than I had imagined.' He paused. 'Now that the first time is out of the way maybe I could come out with you some time.'

'Why not? You could crew for me.' She spoke lightly, but at the thought of sailing with him alone in *Mistral*, at one with the sea and the sky with the sun warm on their shoulders and the taste of salt on their lips, she felt a throb of pure excitement.

Jon waited in the car while she visited the patient, and when she rejoined him he threw her a questioning look.

'Problems?' he asked.

'Not really. He's just had a hip replacement.'

'Wasn't he given analgesics to come home with?' asked Jon.

Kate nodded. 'Yes, but they weren't effective, apparently. I've prescribed something stronger.'

'I see. I thought you had a problem there for a moment—readmission or something.'

'No, nothing like that.' She hesitated. 'Nothing like the problem I shall have tomorrow.'

'Oh?' He threw her a quick glance as she drew away from the kerb. 'What's that?'

'I've received the results from a lumbar puncture on one of my patients—you remember Pete Steel?'

'The paramedic?'

Kate nodded. 'It's not looking good. He came to me a few weeks ago, complaining of numbness and lack of co-ordination. I had my suspicions then but I hoped I might be wrong. I ran all the usual tests and sent him for a lumbar puncture.'

'Are we talking MS here?' asked Jon.

'Yes.' Kate nodded.

'Poor chap. What age is he?'

'Thirty-three. And he's married with children.'

'It'll be the end of his job,' said Jon slowly.

'I know,' said Kate. 'I've been dreading telling him. But I can't put it off any longer.' She sighed. 'We have some frightful things to do sometimes, don't we?'

'You're right there.' He nodded. 'Want me to come along when you tell him? Bit of moral support?'

Kate shook her head. 'No. It's kind of you, Jon, but Pete is my patient. I have to do it. I need to talk to his wife as well.'

'OK, but the offer's still there if you should change your mind.'

'Thanks.' She doubted if she would take him up on it, but somehow it was infinitely comforting to know he was there, offering unseen support. It was a new experience for Kate, but one she decided she could easily get used to.

In fact, the more she came to think of it the more she realised how close they had grown professionally as well as socially, over the past weeks. They had compared case histories, diagnoses and various forms of treatment. Sometimes they argued, or Jon would compare Kate's methods with those he would apply in the bush. More often than not these days they would end up laughing, whereas in the early days their arguments would have left Kate smarting with anger and indignation.

The following afternoon Kate drew up outside Pete and Sue Steel's red-brick semi-detached house, and for a few minutes remained sitting in her car, bracing herself for what she had to do. When she knew she could delay the moment no longer she got out of the car, walked slowly up to the house and rang the doorbell.

Pete himself answered the door.

'Hello, Pete.' Kate managed a bright smile.

'Why, Dr Chapman.' Pete's ready smile and surprise at seeing her was quickly replaced by a look of wariness.

'Can I come in for a moment?' asked Kate.

'Of course.' Pete stood aside.

'Is Sue at home?' Kate stepped into the hall and Pete closed the front door behind her.

'Yes,' he replied, 'she's in the kitchen. I. . .I was just playing football with the boys. I take it you've got something to tell me. . .' He trailed off.

'Yes, Pete, I have,' said Kate gently. 'I've had the results of your lumbar puncture. Do you want Sue with you?'

He nodded, and by the time he had called his wife and they had both joined Kate in the sitting room she had the distinct impression that Pete had worked out exactly what she was going to say. For Sue, however, it came as more of a shock.

'Multiple sclerosis?' she said, horror gathering in her eyes as she stared at Kate.

'There's no cure, is there, Doc?' Pete had walked to the patio window on hearing the diagnosis of his illness and was staring up the garden.

From where Kate was sitting on the settee, she could see the couple's two young sons as they kicked their football. 'Not as such, Pete, no,' she replied truthfully. As his shoulders sagged slightly she added, 'But there is a great deal that can be done these days to help the condition. You may also have long periods of remission where things really don't get any worse.'

'What about his job?' asked Sue suddenly, as if the practicalities of the situation were only just beginning to sink in.

Kate turned and looked at her and saw the fear in her eyes. It was Pete who answered, turning from the window to face the two women. 'They'll kick me out,' he said brutally.

'No.' Sue's hand flew to her mouth. 'Maybe they'll—'

'A disabled paramedic's no use to anyone.' Pete shrugged and turned back to the window.

'The most important thing at this stage is to adopt a positive attitude,' said Kate firmly. 'To establish what you can do rather than what you can't. First of all, Pete, I'd like you to come along to the surgery in the next day or two so that I can do a complete assessment, then we'll talk about drugs and physiotherapy.'

'Should I go to work?' Pete turned again and this time Kate saw the expression in his eyes, one of anger and bitterness rather than of fear.

'I think until we do the assessment it would be better if I were to write you a certificate—just to be on the safe side.' Opening her case, Kate drew out her pad of sickness certificates and began to fill one in. There was complete silence in the room as she wrote. When she had finished she tore off the form, handed it to Pete, then stood up.

'I'm really sorry, Pete, Sue,' she said at last, not wanting to trivialise what had happened in any way but at the same time not wanting either of them to sink into despair. 'I wish I could have brought you better news, I really do.'

It was almost a relief to go, to get away from the pain in their eyes—a pain which nothing she said or did could be alleviated in any way.

'I felt so helpless,' she said later to Jon when she got back to the surgery and he came into her room to ask her how it had gone.

'There's no easy way to tell a man he has something like MS,' said Jon.

'I tried to dwell on the positive side, on what could be done rather than on what he wouldn't be able to do, but. . .' Helplessly she spread her hands.

'Being a paramedic, I would say Pete Steel knows rather more than average.'

Kate nodded, and as Jon was about to leave the room she called him back. 'I haven't seen Helen for the last few days,' she said, adding, 'Has she said how Harry is?'

'Apparently, he hasn't recognised her on the last two occasions she has visited him.'

Kate sighed. 'I fear his deterioration may be more rapid than we had thought.'

At that moment the intercom sounded on Kate's desk. 'Yes, Claire?' she said.

'Is Dr Hammomd with you?' asked Claire.

'He is.'

'We've had an urgent call from Social Services. Apparently, Marion Everton has been picked up by the police in a seafront shelter. She's been drinking again and she's in a bad way. They would like someone to visit. I wasn't sure who would go.'

'I'll go, Claire,' said Jon, leaning forward and speaking

into the intercom. 'Where is she exactly?'

'At the police station,' Claire replied.

'Would you like me to come with you?' Kate stood up as Jon opened the door.

'I dare say I can cope.'

'I'm sure you can. But I may be of some help. I know the family and I'm familiar with the situation.'

'Aren't you busy?' He glanced at the pile of paperwork on her desk.

'I've finished surgery,' she said. 'I don't have any house calls, as far as I know, and as for this—' she indicated the paperwork '—that will always be there.'

'OK. Thanks. I'll be glad of your help.' His eyes met hers and she felt a curious little glow deep inside at the prospect of working alongside him once more. The days had long gone when he'd required help with the computers, and Kate had often found herself regretting their passing.

They took both cars as it was late in the day and each of them would be returning to their own homes after the visit. They were met in the foyer of the local police station by a WPC and the Evertons' social worker, Barbara Westbury. She seemed pleased, if a little surprised, at the presence of two doctors.

'Is Marion in custody?' asked Kate.

'No,' Barbara replied. 'It was just that we had to allow her to sober up somewhere.'

'It was that bad?' asked Jon.

Barbara nodded. 'Afraid so.'

'Do we know what triggered it this time?' asked Kate.

'We're not sure, although her husband, Den, has recently been released from prison. That may have had some bearing on it,' Barbara added.

Kate frowned. 'In the past, it's been Den going to prison that seems to have started Marion's drinking. This sounds as if it might be the opposite way round.'

'Where are the children?' asked Jon.

'We've had to take the younger ones into care.'

'But what about Den? Couldn't he. . .?' Kate glanced from Barbara to the WPC as she saw a look pass between them.

'He's done a bunk,' said the WPC. 'Nowhere to be found.'

'Oh, I see,' said Kate. 'Well, we'd better go and have a word with Marion.'

'There's something else you need to know, Dr Chapman,' said the WPC.

Kate and Jon had been about to follow Barbara down the corridor to the interview rooms but they paused. 'What's that?' asked Kate.

'Marion has a lot of fresh bruising to her face and body. Although she won't admit anything, we think she has been badly beaten up.'

Kate stiffened as a sudden wave of nausea swept over her. Taking a deep breath, she said, 'In that case, we really do need to see her.'

Her thin body wrapped in a shabby duffle coat, Marion Everton sat huddled in one corner of the interview room. The room reeked of alcohol and the stench of vomit. As Jon and Kate sat down at a small wooden table Marion lifted her purple, swollen face.

'Marion.' It was Barbara Westbury who spoke first. 'Dr Chapman and Dr Hammond have come to see you.'

'Dunno what for,' muttered Marion. 'Lot of good they can do.'

'We want to help you, Marion,' said Kate. 'Would you

let me have a look at those bruises on your face?' She glanced at Jon. 'Do you mind?' she said. When he shook his head she moved forward and gently tilted Marion's face to the light so that she could see the full extent of her injuries.

'Who did this to you?' she said quietly.

Marion didn't answer. Instead, she turned her face away from Kate.

'Marion, you must tell us who did this to you.'

'Why?' Marion turned her head again and looked up at Kate with dull, hopeless eyes.

'So that we can help you.'

'I don't want to talk about it,' mumbled Marion.

'I can understand that,' said Kate gently.

Marion had turned away again but she moved her head once more and looked at Kate. 'You reckon?' she said bitterly.

'Yes,' said Kate, 'I reckon.'

'What the hell would you know about it? You with your fancy flat and your money. . .you couldn't even begin to imagine what it's like. Not in a million years you couldn't.' She almost spat it out and there was outright contempt now in Marion Everton's voice.

'Try me.' Kate crouched down in front of Marion, aware that Jon was listening to every word she said and watching every move she made. 'I might just know more than you think.'

Marion frowned, trying to focus on Kate through swollen, puffy eyelids.

'Was it Den?' asked Kate. 'Did he do this to you?'

Marion remained silent but when Kate asked the same question again, more persistently this time, she inclined her head very slightly.

'Has it happened before, Marion? Was this the first time?' This time there was a slight almost imperceptible shake of her head.

'How many times before? Once?' Another shake.

'Many times. Is that it, Marion? Den has battered you many times?'

There was silence in the room, a silence so profound it was almost tangible as they waited for the final, slight nod of confirmation from Marion Everton.

'Well done, Marion.' It was Jon who spoke, breaking that silence. 'The worst part was telling us. Now maybe we can start getting you the help that you need.'

He stood back, obviously assuming that Kate would be the one to examine Marion and assess her injuries as it had been she who had taken the initiative in asking the questions, but suddenly Kate found that she was unable to move. It was as if she were in some way rooted to the spot.

Jon threw her a questioning glance as if he understood, which of course he didn't, and took over Marion Everton's examination.

As he began to list her injuries the WPC took notes while Kate looked on helplessly.

'There is bruising to the left cheek,' said Jon, 'swelling and contusions to the left eye and along the left side of the jawbone. Two teeth are missing.' He turned to Barbara Westbury. 'Would you remove her blouse, please?'

The social worker did as he asked and it was as further severe bruising to Marion's shoulder, ribs and both breasts was revealed, and as very gently Jon began to probe, that Kate felt herself begin to shake. Not the mild sort of trembling which sometimes signifies hunger or tiredness, but a shaking that seemed to come from the very depths of her being.

'Now, Marion,' said Jon, straightening as he completed his examination, 'We are going to get you to Casualty at the Shalbrooke. I want you to have some X-rays—to your jaw and that shoulder—and I would imagine they'll want to keep you overnight. In the meantime, Miss Westbury will arrange for you to go to a women's refuge. Just for the time being,' he said firmly as Marion seemed about to protest, then sank back into apathy.

Somehow Kate got through the formalities and found herself and Jon outside the police station in the car park. She was about to escape to the sanctuary of her car when she felt Jon's hand on her arm. It was almost her undoing and she felt the tears gathering behind her eyelids.

'Kate, are you all right?' His voice was low, concerned, questioning.

'Yes,' she answered sharply. 'Yes, I'm fine. I must go, Jon. I have things to do. I'll see you tomorrow.' Blinded by her tears, she fumbled with the car doorhandle.

Seconds later she shot out of the car park with a squeal of tyres, only too aware that she'd left Jon standing beside his own car on the tarmac and staring after her, his expression a mixture of concern and amazement.

She didn't remember driving home and wasn't sure afterwards how she'd done so, knowing only the intense relief when she reached her apartment. Closing the door behind her weakly, she leaned against it. Shutting her eyes, the tears oozed from beneath her eyelids and trickled unchecked down her cheeks.

What in the world was wrong with her? She really should be over all this by now. Even the fact that what had happened between herself and Alistair was unresolved she had in some way to overcome, because with Alistairs's death it would never *be* resolved. She knew all that and had thought she had been coming to terms with it. If that was the case, why should what had just happened have affected her so much?

It had been seeing Marion Everton that had done it.

Kate's breath caught in a shuddering sob in her throat as an image of Marion's bruised, swollen face floated through her mind. She'd seen women like Marion before, too often in the course of her job, and had spoken to them, counselled them. . .so why now? Why this?

The sudden buzz of the intercom broke into her thoughts, almost frightening her out of her wits. Helplessly she stared at the machine on the wall.

Who was it?

She wasn't expecting anyone. Didn't want to see anyone. Didn't want anyone to see her like this—a quivering, helpless wreck. If she kept quiet perhaps whoever it was would just go away.

The buzzer sounded again. It was longer this time and more persistent, followed almost immediately by a second and then a third buzz.

Whoever it was wasn't going to go away.

Trying to compose herself, Kate lifted the receiver. Even before she had the chance to speak she heard his voice. 'Kate, it's me, Jon. Please let me in.'

She didn't want to see him. She didn't want to see anyone. And Jon Hammond was the very last person she wanted to see her in this state.

'Please, Kate,' he said.

Still she hesitated, then at last, with a sigh, she pressed the button to open the downstairs door to her apartment. He was up the stairs and inside the hallway in a trice.

One look at her tearstained face and shaking hands was enough for Jon, and before she had time even to think what was happening he had gathered her into his arms and was holding her so tightly against him that she could hear his heart pounding.

Surprisingly, it felt very safe there in his arms, and for a long moment she found she was perfectly content to stay there while her tears quietly soaked the front of his shirt.

'Kate,' he whispered against her hair. 'Oh, Kate. I had to come. I was so worried about you. What is it?' Gently he held her away from him and looked down at her. 'What is it?' he said again.

Helplessly, as her tears started afresh, she shook her head. 'I'm not sure I can tell you,' she mumbled, her voice barely coherent as once more she buried her face in his chest.

'Well, I think you have to tell someone, whatever it is,' said Jon at last. 'I think you need to tell either someone who is professionally trained or, on the other hand, someone who really cares for you.' Very gently his fingers found her chin and lifted her face to his once more, equally gently brushing her lips with his own.

'It's a long story,' she said shakily at last, looking up at him as he drew away.

'I'm not going anywhere,' he replied. Taking her hand, he led her into the sitting room and lowered himself onto the sofa. He drew her down beside him, keeping her firmly, safely, within the circle of his arm.

Before them, beyond the vast picture window, the Solent gradually darkened in the gathering twilight. Mainland lights twinkled on the far shores and a flame leapt into the indigo sky from one of Fawley's tall chimneys. A liner slid silently into view on its return from some exotic resort, it's lighted decks like the rooms of a sultan's palace as it glided into Southampton Water.

'I don't know where to start,' said Kate at last.

'I've always been led to believe that the beginning is the best place,' said Jon.

'In that case. . .' Kate took a deep, faltering breath '. . .I guess I need to start with Alistair.'

CHAPTER TWELVE

'So who exactly is Alistair?' asked Jon.

'The man I thought I was going to marry,' Kate replied. 'And it's "was", not "is" by the way—he was killed in a car crash in the States some time ago.'

'I'm sorry,' said Jon.

Kate gave a little shrug. 'These things happen, I guess. . .'

When Jon remained silent but attentive, as if waiting for her to proceed, she took a deep breath and braced herself for what was to come. At the same time she desperately tried to marshal her thoughts into some sort of order so that they wouldn't come out in a dreadful jumble of confusion and emotion.

'I met Alistair Cunningham at a party in London while I was working at Barts,' she said at last. As she started to speak she realised that she'd clenched her fists, that the back of her neck beneath her hair felt uncomfortably damp and that deep inside her the hard knot of fear was still tightly coiled. 'I was immediately attracted to him,' she went on. 'He was young, charming, handsome, witty and he was a high-flier in the legal profession—all the right attributes to attract any girl, I suppose.'

She swallowed, 'Anyway, when he phoned after the party and asked me for a date I didn't hesitate. He took me for dinner at a top London restaurant. Afterwards, we danced. I knew very early on that he was attracted to me. . .he made that very plain.

174

We continued to date for some time...several months, in fact...I took him to meet my parents and I met his sister. His parents were dead. He...' She paused and realised that as she had been talking her fists had uncurled. 'He was everything I had ever wanted in a man, so much so that quite early on in our relationship we moved into a flat together...'

'Where had you been living before that?' asked Jon.

'Oh, I had been sharing a house with two other girls and Alistair had been sharing a flat with a colleague. By then we had talked of marriage, of having children... everything...so it seemed inevitable that we should get a place together. Somehow, that's what made what followed so much harder to believe...'

Taking one of her hands where it lay in her lap, Jon gently began to caress it with his thumb. 'The death of a loved one is always difficult to come to terms with...' he said at last, 'but if you can bring yourself to talk about it...it really will help.'

Kate frowned. Sharply she lifted her head and stared at Jon.

'Oh, it's not Alistairs's death that I've had difficulty coming to terms with,' she said at last. 'It's what happened before that.'

'What do you mean?' It was Jon's turn to frown.

'It...it was what happened before...before we split up.' By now the palms of her hands were quite damp. Carefully she wiped them down her skirt before Jon retrieved the one he'd been holding.

'Can you tell me about it?' said Jon quietly.

'I think I have to,' she replied shakily. 'seeing the state I'm in. I guess the time has come.'

She paused, rearranging the terrifying memories into

order and at the same time calming, then steeling herself at last to face the inevitable moment which has been delayed for so long—the moment that would hopefully, eventually, lead to peace and healing.

As she began to speak Jon's arm tightened around her while he continued to caress her hand, soothing and encouraging her.

'At first everything was wonderful,' she said, 'even though quite early on I had become aware of a possessive streak in Alistair. At the time I didn't think it posed too much of a problem. It was confined to quite ordinary things—you know the sort of thing. Referring to the flat as his flat when by then it was our home, to our belongings as his—his stereo, his CD's, that sort of thing.'

'Did that bother you?' asked Jon curiously.

'No. Not really.' Kate shook her head. 'I was so in love with him by that time I really didn't care, especially over something I considered to be so trivial. But. . .as time went on I gradually realised that this possessiveness included me. I began to find this more difficult to accept, I must confess. I had always been fiercely independent and this was something very alien to me.'

'Did you tackle him about it?'

'Only half-heartedly. Again, I guess I was so in love with him I was prepared to overlook this trait in his character. At that time that is all I thought it was—a trait or a quirk, nothing more. I should have known, of course. My training alone should have warned me. But it didn't, I suppose because I didn't want to see it.' She stopped again and in the sudden silence in the room the only sounds to be heard were the ticking of the clock on the mantelpiece and outside the muted, low roar of the sea.

'Unfortunately,' Kate went on at last, 'I also didn't see

the jealousy that was beneath the possessiveness. There were a few small incidents that again should have warned me—but I ignored them because I didn't want to know.'

'Can you say what sort of incidents?' said Jon softly.

'The usual things. He always wanted a blow-by-blow account of my day. Where I'd been, who I'd been with—you know the kind of thing. At first I was flattered. No one had ever taken that much interest in me before. But then. . .then it got a bit awkward. His questioning began to include my patients, and on more than one occasion I found myself right on the brink of breaking confidentiality just to keep Alistair satisfied. I never did, but it was a hard job making him understand.'

'But surely as a lawyer. . .'

'I know. Sounds ludicrous, doesn't it? But there it was.' She gave a shrug. 'There was a curious little-boy side to Alistair,' she continued after a moment. 'It was completely separate from his role as a barrister, but it was something that needed constant attention.'

'Anyway. . .one day. . .' She paused, hesitating. 'One day something happened, something that should have been enough to warn me. It was one afternoon. I'd come back to the flat unexpectedly. I had some time off. By some coincidence Alistair had finished work early as well and he arrived home just after me. We decided to make use of this unexpected time together in the usual way. It was wonderful, as our lovemaking always was. Then. . . then, afterwards. . .he. . .he began to question me. . .'

'To question you?' prompted Jon when for the moment Kate fell silent.

'Yes,' she replied. He wanted to know why I had returned to the flat—his flat, as he called it—in the middle of the afternoon. At first I laughed, tried to make some

light-hearted joke. . .then I realised that he was implying
that I had come back to meet someone else there. Still I
tried to turn it into a joke but I quickly realised that he
was deadly serious. I tried to reason with him, even
pointing out that I could think the same thing of him as
he, too, had come home early.'

'And. . .?' said Jon.

'He totally ignored that. His questioning went on and
on. In the end he was demanding to know the name of
the person. Was even asking if I'd met him before. If I'd
made love with him. Asking what it had been like. If the
man was better in bed than he was.

'By then I was so angry I got out of bed, left him there
and went into the bathroom. I had just started to run a
bath. I turned to get some bath foam from the cupboard.
Alistair was there. He. . .he had come into the bathroom,
without my hearing him. He. . .he hit me. Punched me. . .
here below my shoulder. The force and the element of
surprise pushed me backwards and I fell against the bath,
banging my head on the rim and cutting it. I was so
shocked I simply sat there on the floor, staring up at him.
The next thing I knew he was down beside me and wiping
the blood from my face—holding me and telling me how
sorry he was.'

There was silence in the room again. Gently, Jon said,
'And was he sorry?'

'At the time, yes. I really believe he was,' said Kate.
'He said it over and over again. Begged me to forgive
him. And, because I loved him so much, of course I did.
He swore it would never happen again and I believed
him. . .because I wanted to believe him. Again, at the
time I think he meant it.'

'He probably did,' said Jon. 'Until the next time.' When

Kate remained silent he said. 'I take it there was a next time?'

'Oh, yes,' she said, 'there was a next time. Of course there was a next time. I have to say, it didn't happen for a long time—almost a year, in fact, during which time we were making plans for our wedding. It happened at Christmas, after a party on one of the wards. I hadn't had much to drink but I decided it was enough to maybe put me over the limit to drive. I was about to phone for a cab when another doctor, Jim Naylor, a guy I'd trained with, offered to run me home. I accepted, without thinking.

'It was quite late when we got to the flat. I invited Jim inside for a coffee. I suppose by then I was beginning to be wary, knowing that Alistair was home and would want to know how I had got home. He was perfectly charming to Jim. Even made the coffee and chatted about Christmas arrangements.

'He fooled even me, Jon.' Her voice faltered and Jon drew her even closer.

'This time there was no questioning,' she went on after a moment. 'He hit me as soon as he'd closed the front door. Jim was still outside in his car. . . He hit me again and again. . .' She began to sob, great searing sobs that seemed to come from her very soul. 'Then. . .then he dragged me. . .by my hair. . .it was long in those days. . . he dragged me into the bedroom and forced me to. . . to. . .you know. . .on the floor. . .not even on the bed.'

'He raped you,' said Jon.

'Not really,' said Kate, noticing that this time it was Jon's hand which had clenched into a fist. 'I had been living with him. . .'

'But he forced you?'

'Oh, yes. It was the last thing I wanted at that moment.'

'He raped you,' said Jon.

'Yes.' Kate gave a great, shuddering sigh.

'Yes,' she said again. 'Then he carried on beating me. I thought. . .I thought I was going to die. . .'

Turning her face, wet now with tears, she buried it in Jon's shirt and while he held her she sobbed out the storm of her anger and her fear.

Later she lay quietly in the circle of his arms and continued her story.

'I left him immediately—the very next day. I moved into accommodation at the hospital. I had recently received a letter from Richard Fleetwood, asking me if I would consider a partnership in the practice. At the time I had turned it down, believing my future lay in London with Alistair and possibly training for a consultancy. Now I saw it as my salvation.

'I rang Richard and asked if the post was still open. When he said it was and that they would be delighted to have me I handed in my notice at Barts. I had leave owing so I was able to leave immediately. I travelled down to Dorset and stayed with my parents for a couple of weeks, before moving to the Island.'

'You didn't go to the police?'

'No.' Kate shook her head. 'No, I know I should have done,' she said quietly, 'but somehow I just couldn't face it. I didn't think anyone would believe me. Everyone liked Alistair, you see. . .he was so charming. . .and what with him being a lawyer and everything. . .'

'So you told no one?'

Kate hesitated. 'I told some of it to a female colleague at Barts who didn't know Alistair. I showed her my injuries.'

'What did she say?'

'She tried to persuade me to go to the police. But I couldn't. . .'

And what of Cunningham? Did he leave you alone?'

'No. Not immediately. At first he begged me to go back and tried all the old tricks—said how sorry he was, how it wouldn't happen again. He even followed me to Dorset. In the end I told him that I'd told a colleague what he'd done and that she'd witnessed my injuries. I said that if he didn't leave me alone I was going to the police.'

'Did it work?'

'Not straight away. He was very persistent. Then, right out of the blue, I heard he'd gone to the States. I was so relieved that I guess I tried to blot the whole thing out of my mind.'

'You never spoke of it again?'

Kate shook her head. 'No. I know now that I should have done, just as I know I should have reported him— but it seemed as if I had some sort of mental block where he was concerned.' She paused again reflectively.

'I was dreadfully shocked when I heard he had been killed,' she continued after a while, 'but I still seemed incapable of facing it. Eventually every memory of him became locked up, along with the terror.'

'Until now,' said Jon softly.

'Yes,' Kate agreed, 'until now. It was seeing Marion Everton like that that did it. Something just seemed to explode—it was like a dam bursting. Once it had gone the flood just came and went on and on—'

'You'll be much better for it, you know. . .'

'Yes. I know.' She stopped again biting her lip. 'I thought I'd come to terms with it, you know. But I hadn't. I never really trusted anyone, you see.'

'I know that,' said Jon. 'You certainly didn't trust me when I stayed here.'

'I know I didn't.'

'Not that I can blame you under the circumstances. What happened to you is enough to make anyone wary. . . But we aren't all like him, you know, Kate.'

While they had been talking he had been playing with a strand of her hair, twisting it round his finger. Now he tugged it gently, tilting her face so that she was forced to look up at him.

'I know that,' she whispered.

'Maybe now you will feel it's time to move on, time to give someone else a chance.'

She sighed. 'Yes, maybe. You know something, Jon? For a long time I had convinced myself I would never become romantically involved with anyone ever again and then. . .then one day this off-beat guy with tatty jeans and a lopsided smile sauntered into my life and everything changed.'

He chuckled. 'So you think this guy might be in with a chance?'

'He may well be.' Kate gave a deep sigh and snuggled down deeper into Jon's arms. 'He may well be.'

She was falling in love with him. As May unfolded and tumbled into summer, as the candles on the horse chestnuts burst forth in a blaze of pink or white and blossom thick as whipped cream topped the blackthorn hedgerows, Kate came to know that she would never find a more gentle man anywhere in the world. Tough and hard-bitten might be the exterior he presented, but she quickly found the infinite tenderness that dwelt within.

Not once did he force any issue, content, it seemed, to

wait as she faced, and, with his help, dealt with the demons that had assailed her for so long.

More and more time was spent in each other's company as they learnt all there was to know, and while he helped her with her traumas, she in turn listened as he released the pain of his childhood. Many times they talked far into the night, forgetting the lateness of the hour, and while their love remained unconsummated the trust between them grew as they simply held each other in the darkness.

For Kate there was still some part of her that held back from committing herself entirely to Jon. She had committed herself to Alistair and it had all gone so terribly wrong. Whereas she had no such fears about Jon, there was a part of her that knew that if she made another such commitment she would be utterly devastated after his return to Africa.

And then one day everything changed.

It had been a particularly busy day at the surgery—a day of long consultations, numerous house calls, a practice meeting and extra clinics for them both—a day after which both of them returned to Kate's apartment and collapsed in relief onto the sofa.

Afterwards when she tried to recall the sequence of events Kate was at a loss to do so for what happened seemed totally spontaneous and within the natural order of things.

At first they simply found themselves in each other's arms, but as that had become such a regular occurence these days it alone didn't hold special significance.

Then somehow their kisses grew deeper and more passionate, and as they both became increasingly aroused they moved into the bedroom where Jon sat beside her on the bed and gently undid the buttons on her blouse then slipped the silky material from her shoulders.

She watched him as he discarded his own clothes, loving him, loving every line of his lean but powerful body—the skin, bronzed by the Tanzanian sun, the gold-tipped hair, the muscles that rippled across back and shoulders—and when at last he stretched out above her and she looked up into those grey eyes she also loved the expression she saw there for it reflected her own love for him.

In the past few years Kate had come to doubt that she would ever again experience the moment when a man took possession of her body. Now, with Jon, she knew no fear. In spite of his obvious arousal and his overwhelming need for her, he held back, making certain she, too, was ready. He caressed and aroused her with mouth and fingertips until in the end it was she who begged him for release.

He was gentle at first, but as her passion flared to match his own his desire, controlled for so long, seemed to explode along with hers in a fury of such sweetness that left Kate helpless and almost delirious with joy.

She clung to him for a long time afterwards as if she could not bear to ever let him go.

'I love you, Kate,' he murmured in the tangle of her hair.

'I love you too.' She stretched languourously, flinging her arms wide. 'That was wonderful,' she sighed. 'Quite, quite wonderful.'

Supporting himself on one elbow, he smiled teasingly down at her. 'You said that as if it was over.'

'Isn't it?' She raised one eyebrow but under the light sheet, which he had pulled up to cover them both, she moved her hips slightly so that they rubbed against him.

'I can assure you,' he replied, 'I've only just begun.'

'Really?' Her eyes widened innocently. 'Let's hope neither of us gets called out, then.'

'Will Helen wonder why you haven't come home?' she asked him later, much later.

'I shouldn't think so,' he replied. 'She knows I'm a big boy and perfectly able to take of myself.'

'I just thought she might worry—might think you'd been involved in an accident, that's all.'

'You think I should phone her?'

'It might be an idea. She may just start calling the hospital or even phoning the police. On the other hand. . .' she smiled mischieviously at him '. . .maybe you're embarrassed at telling Helen where you are.'

'Me? Embarrassed?' He grinned lazily but made no effort to move.

'Come on, I'll do it.' Leaning across him, she picked up the telephone and dialled Helen's number. Helen answered on the third ring.

'Hello, Helen—it's Kate. Sorry it's so late—hope you weren't in bed.'

'No, not yet. Richard's only just gone. What can I do for you, Kate?'

'Nothing, really. I was only phoning to say that Jon won't be home tonight, that's all.'

There was silence on the other end of the line, then Helen said, 'Is that so?'

'Yes,' Kate replied, arching her back as she suddenly felt Jon's hand move slowly across her stomach and cup her breast. 'We. . .I . . . thought you might worry or think he might have had an accident or something. . .'

'When in fact he's simply there with you—is that it?' Helen gave a chuckle.

'Something like that, yes,' Kate replied, her breath catching in her throat in a suppressed gasp as with firm, circular movements of his thumb and fingers Jon began caressing her again.

'Well, I'm delighted to hear it,' said Helen. 'I didn't think the pair of you were ever going to get around to it. And while we're on the subject maybe this could be the answer to another little problem.'

'Oh,' said Kate, 'and what's that?' Out of the corner of her eye she saw that Jon had raised his head and was obviously trying to fathom out what was being said. His hand, however, continued its devastating work.

'I had a phone call this evening from my cousin's daughter, Siobhan. Her training finishes in about three weeks' time.'

'So she'll be wanting to move into the flat?'

'Yes. I was getting a bit concerned where Jon was going to go, especially with the season getting under way. Looks like I've been worrying for nothing.'

'Maybe you have, Helen.' With a laugh Kate replaced the receiver.

'Am I being evicted?' asked Jon, pausing for a moment in the rhythm of his movements.

'Sounds like it,' Kate replied.

'Looks like I shall have to start looking around for somewhere to live,' he said seriously.

'Short-term lets are difficult to find.'

'Who said anything about short term?' he said as she moved closer to him again and he continued with what he had been doing.

Kate stared at him. 'Well, I didn't think you'd be staying after Paul returns.'

'Why not?'

'Well, your work with the VSO—won't you be returning to Tanzania?'

'Maybe not.' He shrugged slightly and Kate's heart gave a sudden lurch. 'I think maybe the time has come to hang up my bush hat and put down some roots in this country,' he said.

'But what about a job?'

'Shouldn't be too difficult. I spoke to Richard the other day and he said there are usually plenty of jobs going at the Shalbrooke.'

'You'd go back to hospital work?' She stared at him in astonishment.

'Until something else comes along—yes.' He nodded and smiled down at her, that crazy, lopsided smile of his that she had so come to love.

'But you love Africa,' she protested. 'You told me once that it was your whole life and that it would take something very special to make you give it up.'

'Maybe I've found that something special,' he said lazily.

'You mean. . .?' Still she stared up at him, hardly able to believe what she was hearing.

'Yes, Kate. You're that something special I was talking about. I suspected it the moment I set eyes on you, in spite of that haughty look you gave me when you realised I was the new locum and not that stuffed shirt of a medical rep. No, don't bother to deny it,' he said as she opened her mouth to protest, 'because it's absolutely true. You really didn't like me to start with, and I can't say I altogether blame you. I really wasn't quite what you were used to.'

'You were. . .unconventional,' she admitted at last.

'I guess that's one word for it.' He grinned. 'But it

doesn't alter the fact that you were definitely unimpressed...whereas for me...well, very early on I was quite smitten by this lovely but untouchable lady, and within a very short space of time I knew you were the one who was about to turn my world upside down.'

'I thought you'd think I was frigid,' she said, looking away, unable to meet his eyes. 'Especially after that night at the stable flat.'

'I must admit I was puzzled,' he said, 'but I came to the conclusion there had to be a reason because I was certain that underneath all that there was a warm, passionate woman—and I was right.'

Even as she lay there, almost too stunned to think straight, he moved, covering her body again with his own.

'You're definitely my something special, Kate.' His voice was husky now with emotion, his eyes dark with desire as he gazed down at her.

'And you'd do that for me—give up Africa and the VSO?'

'Sure. Like I said, it's time I put some roots down. I guess I dipped out on the family bit when I was a kid so it's more than time I made up for it.' He paused as a glint of amusement entered his eyes, and added, 'But there's something I need to ask of you in return.'

'Of course,' she said, thinking for one moment that he was going to ask if she would consider going to Africa with him at some point in the future and knowing that at that moment she would agree to almost anything.

'Do you think we could please stop talking now?' he said. 'Because if we don't I'm going to be in big trouble.'

'Oh, Jon.' With a laugh and a sigh of delicious anticipation, Kate wound her arms around his neck and drew him down to her again.

MILLS & BOON®

Medical Romance™

COMING NEXT MONTH

PRECIOUS OFFERINGS by Abigail Gordon

Springfield Community Hospital ... meeting old friends

Rafe was sure that Lucinda couldn't be immune to his charm; after all she was only human; now all he had to do was get her to admit it!

DR McIVER'S BABY by Marion Lennox

Kids & Kisses ... another heart-warming story

Marriage of convenience was definitely the wrong word. Looking after Tom, his baby and his two dogs, Annie thought it must be madness—or was it love?

A CHANCE IN A MILLION by Alison Roberts

It was ancient history. The last time that Fee had seen Jon Fletcher he'd been about to get married and live on the other side of the world. But now he was back and minus a wife...

SOMETHING SPECIAL by Carol Wood

Sam had only one thought on the subject of career women—avoid them at all cost! But getting to know Paula, he was beginning to think he may have been wrong.

On Sale from 4th May 1998

DEBBIE MACOMBER

The Playboy and the Widow

A confirmed bachelor, Cliff Howard wasn't prepared to
trade in the fast lane for car pools. Diana Collins lived life
hiding behind motherhood and determined to play it
safe. They were both adept at playing their roles.
Until the playboy met the widow...

"Debbie Macomber's stories sparkle with love and laughter..."
—*New York Times* bestselling author, Jayne Ann Krentz

MIRA®

1-55166-080-6
AVAILABLE FROM MAY 1998

DANCE FEVER

How would you like to win a year's supply of Mills & Boon® books? Well you can and they're FREE! Simply complete the competition below and send it to us by 31st October 1998. The first five correct entries picked after the closing date will each win a year's subscription to the Mills & Boon series of their choice. What could be easier?

OBLARMOL
AMBUR
RTOXTFO
RASQUE
GANCO

KOPLA
OOOOMTLCIN
MALOENCF
SITWT
LASSA

EVJI
TAZLW
ACHACH
SCDIO
MAABS

G	R	I	H	C	H	A	R	J	T	O	N
O	P	A	R	L	H	U	B	P	I	B	W
M	O	O	R	L	L	A	B	M	C	V	H
B	L	D	I	O	O	K	C	L	U	P	E
R	K	U	B	N	C	R	Q	H	V	R	Z
S	A	N	I	O	O	N	G	W	A	S	V
T	S	I	N	R	M	G	E	U	B	G	H
W	L	G	H	S	O	R	Q	M	M	B	L
I	A	P	N	O	T	S	L	R	A	H	C
S	S	L	U	K	I	A	S	F	S	L	S
T	O	R	T	X	O	F	O	X	T	R	F
G	U	I	P	Z	N	D	I	S	C	O	Q

D8C

Please turn over for details of how to enter ⇨

HOW TO ENTER

There is a list of fifteen mixed up words overleaf, all of which when unscrambled spell popular dances. When you have unscrambled each word, you will find them hidden in the grid. They may appear forwards, backwards or diagonally. As you find each one, draw a line through it. Find all fifteen and fill in the coupon below then pop this page into an envelope and post it today. Don't forget you could win a year's supply of Mills & Boon® books—you don't even need to pay for a stamp!

Mills & Boon Dance Fever Competition
FREEPOST CN81, Croydon, Surrey, CR9 3WZ

EIRE readers send competition to PO Box 4546, Dublin 24.

Please tick the series you would like to receive if you are one of the lucky winners

Presents™ ❏   Enchanted™ ❏   Medical Romance™ ❏

Historical Romance™ ❏   Temptation® ❏

Are you a Reader Service™ subscriber?   Yes ❏   No ❏

Ms/Mrs/Miss/Mr ....Intials ....
(BLOCK CAPITALS PLEASE)

Surname..

Address ....

....

....Postcode...........................

(I am over 18 years of age)   D8C

Closing date for entries is 31st October 1998.
One application per household. Competition open to residents of the UK and Ireland only. You may be mailed with offers from other reputable companies as a result of this application. If you would prefer not to receive such offers, please tick this box. ❏

Mills & Boon is a registered trademark of Harlequin Mills & Boon Ltd.